PRAISE FOR THE JAMIE JOHNSON SERIES

"You'll read this and want to get out there and play"
Steven Gerrard

"An inspiring read for all football fans"
Gary Lineker

"If you like football, this book's for you"
Frank Lampard

"Jamie could go all the way"
Jermain Defoe

"I love reading about football and it
doesn't get much better than this"
Joe Hart

"Pure joy"
The Times

"Inspiring"
Observer

"Gripping"
Sunday Express

"A resounding victory"
Telegraph

ABOUT THE AUTHOR

Dan Freedman grew up wanting to be a professional footballer. That didn't happen. But he went on to become a top football journalist, personally interviewing the likes of Cristiano Ronaldo, Lionel Messi, David Beckham and Sir Alex Ferguson. He uses his passion and knowledge of football to write the hugely popular series of Jamie Johnson football novels. When he is not writing, Dan delivers talks and workshops for schools. And he still plays football whenever he can.

www.danfreedman.co.uk
Follow Dan on Twitter @DanFreedman99

For Musashi!
Top Skills!

DAN FREEDMAN

Skills from Brazil

SCHOLASTIC

First published in the UK in 2014 by Scholastic Children's Books
An imprint of Scholastic Ltd
Euston House, 24 Eversholt Street
London, NW1 1DB, UK
Registered office: Westfield Road, Southam, Warwickshire, CV47 0RA
SCHOLASTIC and associated logos are trademarks and/or registered
trademarks of Scholastic Inc.

ISBN 978 1407 14789 5

A CIP catalogue record for this book is available from the British Library.

Printed and bound by CPI Group (UK) Ltd, Croydon, CR0 4YY.
Papers used by Scholastic Children's Books are made from wood
grown in sustainable forests.

1 3 5 7 9 10 8 6 4 2

This is a work of fiction. Names, characters, places, incidents and dialogues are
products of the author's imagination or are used fictitiously. Any resemblance to
actual people, living or dead, events or locales is entirely coincidental.

www.scholastic.co.uk

A press conference is being held at Hawkstone United's stadium.

A smartly dressed man walks through the door and into the room. It is full of photographers and journalists all there to hear what he has to say.

The man sits down at the table and clears his throat. He knows what he is going to say. He prepared these words all of last night. He has been preparing for this moment his entire life.

He pulls the microphone towards him and begins to speak.

"I want to say what an honour it is to be managing in the Premier League and, in particular, here at Hawkstone United," he explains.

His voice is cool, crisp, clear and confident.

"This, for me, is a dream come true."

Part
One

(1)

What Makes You So Special?

Tuesday 29 April

"Jamie Johnson!" Mr Pratley shouted, his hot, smelly coffee breath roaring like a dirty hurricane into Jamie's face.

He had grabbed Jamie's scribbled formation of a Hawkstone United team with all his favourite players and, of course, *J Johnson* as number 11, the left-winger.

This was far from the first time that Jamie had been caught playing fantasy football instead of listening. When it came to football, Jamie's brain was like a powerful computer, working out teams, angles, shots and passes ... but when it came to listening to Pratley,

3

well, Jamie just seemed to switch off as soon as the man started talking. It drove Pratley wild with rage.

"Have you any idea how many boys have been through this school and claimed that they were going to be a footballer when they grew up? Hundreds ... thousands!"

Mr Pratley was now tearing up Jamie's sheet into as many little pieces as possible. The more he ripped the page into smaller and smaller sections, the redder his face became and the wider his eyes bulged.

Jamie did not respond. He couldn't. It was taking every ounce of his power not to burst into laughter. All he could do was stare at the big green bogey that was hovering, tantalizingly loose, from the end of Mr Pratley's nostril. It was a beauty: wet and sticky yet still hard enough to be absolutely ripe for the picking.

"And of those thousands of boys," Pratley continued, the redness now rising from his face into his big, shiny, balding head, "... who ALL thought they were going to be a professional football player ... who ALL thought they were God's gift to the game – just like you no doubt do – have you any idea how many of them did it? How many of them became footballers?"

Jamie shook his head. He'd noticed that the more Pratley was getting worked up and the louder he shouted, the more the bogey had begun to wobble. It was as though it was dancing to the beat of Pratley's anger.

Pratley walked to the front of the classroom and chucked the remnants of Jamie's sheet into the bin. Then he turned and marched back towards Jamie.

The closer he got, the better the view Jamie had of the bogey. It was now doing something amazing. When Pratley breathed out, the bogey poked further out of his nose, as if it were waving to the world. And when he breathed in, it returned slightly further back up his nostril. It appeared to be on some kind of invisible string.

"None!!" barked Pratley. "Not one of those boys became professional footballers! So, I would like you to tell me why you think you are any different."

Jamie looked at his best friend, Jacqueline – or, Jack, as everyone knew her – for help. She shook her head. *Don't talk back*. That's what she was saying to him with her eyes. And she was right. This was a regular occurrence between Jamie and Mr Pratley. For some reason, Jamie had the ability to wind up Pratley more than any other kid in the whole school. The kids found it hysterical but right now, they had reached the danger zone; one more word from Jamie and Pratley might just explode.

Of course there were plenty of things Jamie could

have said; lots of arguments he could have put forward to explain why he believed that, one day, he would become a professional footballer: that he was by far the best player in the school ... that he got all his talent from his granddad, who, had it not been for the injury, would easily have been one of Hawkstone's greatest-ever players ... that he trained and practised every single day because he wanted to become not *just* a professional footballer but one of the best players in the world...

But he didn't say anything. Jack was right. They both knew that whenever Jamie answered back, it only made Pratley even angrier. The best course of action Jamie could take now would be to say nothing. Nothing at all.

And so Jamie just shrugged his shoulders and stayed quiet.

"Answer me, Johnson!" yelled Pratley. "Or I'll keep you in here for the whole of lunchtime by yourself. What makes you think you're so special? What makes you think you've got something that all the other boys didn't?"

Pratley's face was now just an inch from Jamie's. The bogey was smack bang in front of Jamie's eyes. It was moving in and out of the teacher's nose, perfectly in time with Pratley's pants of fury.

Out of the corner of his eye, Jamie saw Jack turn

away. Her body was chugging. She had seen it too and had started laughing without making any noise.

Jamie could feel it coming inside him too. It was rising up through his body like an unstoppable river from his lungs, into his throat and now it was at his mouth. The laughter could not be controlled for very much longer.

"For the very last time, Johnson! Why do you think you are better than any of them?"

"I don't know..." Jamie finally stuttered. The laughter was already leaking out. He knew he was going to get into trouble anyway, so he thought he might as well make it worth it. "*Snot* really for me to say!"

2

The Day of Destiny

"We'll know tomorrow!" shouted Jack, grabbing Jamie by his shirt and dragging him out of lunch.

"Know what?" he asked, laughing as she tugged him all the way to the Assembly Hall.

"TOMORROW!" she repeated, pushing him face to face with the sheet of paper that announced their day of destiny.

Teachers v Pupils

Football Match

The date for this game
has been confirmed!

All details will be
announced in assembly tomorrow

Jamie stared at the notice.

It concerned the football match that he had being looking forward to all year. The match between the teachers of Wheatlands School and the pupils of Year 6. The match that was going to be the biggest of Jamie's life.

Jamie and Jack gazed at the Wheatlands School Football Trophy. Gleaming like treasure, it stood, as always, in its special cabinet in the Assembly Hall. It remained there for the whole year until, on the day of the game itself, the head teacher, Mr Karenza, removed the prize from the cabinet and handed it to the winning captain to lift into the air.

Since they had joined the school, Jamie and Jack had been forced to watch, helpless from the sidelines, as the previous Year 6 pupils' teams had suffered embarrassing losses at the hands of the teachers.

But this year Jamie and Jack were in Year 6. Now it was their chance to play and put things right ... to finally put one over on the teachers.

They had promised themselves that, in this game, things would be different ... that this would be *their* year.

However, just one look at the wooden board – upon which was engraved the results of all the previous matches – spelled out the difficulty of the task that lay ahead.

And it also named the teacher who would be standing in their way.

Teachers V Pupils
The Results

Teachers 11 – 8 Pupils	Winning Captain: C Pratley
Teachers 6 – 4 Pupils	Winning Captain: C Pratley
Teachers 4 – 4 Pupils	Match abandoned
Teachers 8 – 1 Pupils	Winning Captain: C Pratley
Teachers 7 – 3 Pupils	Winning Captain: C Pratley
Teachers 5 – 2 Pupils	Winning Captain: C Pratley
Teachers 9 – 6 Pupils	Winning Captain: C Pratley
Teachers 5 – 3 Pupils	Winning Captain: C Pratley
Teachers 7 – 6 Pupils	Winning Captain: C Pratley
Teachers 6 – 4 Pupils	Winning Captain: C Pratley
Teachers – Pupils	Winning Captain:

3

10,000 Hours

"Come on then," said Jack. "Spit it out."

She and Jamie were walking back home from school together, as they did every day, kicking an old drink can between them along the street.

Jamie shook his head. Sometimes, he didn't like to talk. Even to Jack.

"Look," she said. "You always tell me eventually, so why don't we just skip past the silent bit and get to the talking bit?"

Jamie stared at her. Jack constantly surprised and impressed him. It had been the same since the day he'd met her. They had played football and he had thought that, because she was a girl, she might not be that good. Instead she had proved to be one of the best goalkeepers he had ever seen! Since that day, they had been pretty much inseparable, and sometimes Jamie felt that Jack knew him better than he knew himself.

"It's that stuff Pratley was saying today," he began. "That I'm no different to all the other kids that wanted to be footballers and didn't make it... I know I was laughing and stuff, but I can't get it out of my head."

"You're not still worried about Pratley, are you?" she said. "Just because he's a teacher doesn't mean he knows everything. My dad always says that the people that make the rules aren't any better than the rest of us."

"Yeah," said Jamie. "But what if Pratley's actually right? What if I am no better than the others?"

"OK. So what are you going to do about it?" Jack responded immediately.

"What?" said Jamie. He was shocked by her abruptness and missed his kick of the can.

"Well, you can either keep worrying about it, thinking you're no better than everyone else, or you can start making it happen ... doing something to give yourself that extra edge."

Jamie smiled at her. Jack was the cleverest person he knew but he had no idea what she was going on about.

"How many hours did your granddad Mike say you'd

have to practise if you wanted to become a professional footballer?" she asked.

"Ten thousand," said Jamie. It was one of the many pieces of advice Mike had given him about football. He'd said that the top players only looked so good because they had practised so long and from a very young age.

Ten thousand hours seemed a huge amount to reach but, for Jamie, every second playing football was pure joy.

"Cool," said Jack, flicking the can into the air. "So let's get to the park and get practising!"

And with that she volleyed the can all the way over to the other side of the street, where it looped perfectly into a nearby skip.

Jamie breathed a little more easily. He still felt hurt and worried by Pratley's comments but, at the same time, having Jack's support always gave him a lift.

Jamie was an electrifyingly quick left winger and Jack was a brave and athletic goalkeeper. Together they made a pretty good pair, which was lucky because they both knew that, if they were going to stand any chance of beating the teachers and claiming that gleaming trophy at the end of the year, they would need to be part of the best pupils' team in the history of Wheatlands School.

4
The Announcement

Wednesday 30 April

"And now we move on to the details of the Teachers v Pupils Football Match," announced the head teacher, Mr Karenza, towards the end of assembly the next morning.

Jamie and Jack, who had been kicking each other playfully while Mr Karenza was talking about boring matters, suddenly stopped and sat up at their most alert.

"The match will take place on Thursday, the seventeenth of July, kicking off at two-fifteen p.m.," explained Mr Karenza. "It should be a great way to end the school year, so remember to invite your parents and guardians."

Jamie felt his stomach squirm. Parents. The word made him uncomfortable. There was no way his dad would be turning up to watch – Jamie didn't know how to get in touch with him, even if he wanted to … but at least he would have his mum and his granddad Mike there. Mike was Jamie's biggest fan and, although she knew nothing about football, Jamie's mum had promised to come and watch the game too because she knew how important it was to Jamie.

For a second, he allowed himself to imagine lifting the trophy and running over to show it to her. It would make her so proud.

"I'll referee the game as usual," continued Mr Karenza. "And Mr Pratley, who, as you know, remains unbeaten, will once again captain the teachers' side. Next week, we will hold a vote for all of Year 6 to see who you want to be captain of the pupils…"

Jack kicked Jamie in the shins and smiled at him. Everyone fully expected Jamie to be named captain of the pupils' team. He was the best player in the school and their greatest hope of ending the teachers' winning streak.

Jamie looked at Mr Pratley, who was smirking confidently. Although Jamie and the other kids laughed at him when he lost his temper in lessons, they didn't laugh at him when it came to football. Pratley was

16

a good player and he was ultra-competitive. He had celebrated after the previous years' matches as though he had just won the World Cup Final. This game was just as important to him as it was to the kids.

"Oh, and one final bit of news for you all," Mr Karenza added, looking up and staring at the pupils in a way that made Jamie catch his breath. "Next week, we will be having a new boy joining Year 6. It's late in the year for him to be doing so but there are special circumstances – the boy's father is coming over from abroad to help design the new shopping complex in the centre of Hawkstone. In any case, I hope you will all make him very welcome.

"In fact, I suspect he may very well have a big role to play in the football match too because the boy who is about join our school comes from the world capital of football … Brazil!"

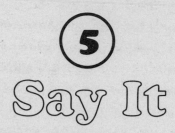

Say It

Friday 2 May

"This guy Pratley is clearly just jealous of your talent, JJ," said Mike Johnson. "Forget him and what he said."

It was Friday night and, as Jamie's mum had a double night-shift at the hospital, Jamie was staying at Mike's. It was good timing because Jamie had a few things on his mind, and Mike – Jamie called him that rather than "Granddad" because they were more like best mates than relatives – always seemed to give the best advice.

It was only now that they had finished dinner – Mike had made Jamie his speciality: toasted cheese sandwiches, brimming with hot melted cheese – that Jamie had opened up and told him about one of the problems he was trying to deal with.

Jamie shrugged. Pratley had made him feel stupid for believing he was different, that he could make it as a professional. And despite what Mike had said, Jamie couldn't just forget it.

"Come on, JJ. Tell me," said Mike, wrapping his big, bearlike arm around Jamie. Sometimes Jamie wondered if he might be the strongest granddad in the world. "What do you want from your life? Everyone wants something. What do you want?"

Jamie shook his head defiantly. In the past he would have answered, quick as a flash: "To be a professional footballer!"

However, now that he really thought about it and considered all the kids in the world who wanted to be professional footballers compared to the number who actually achieved it, Jamie realized how the odds were stacked against him. Statistically, no matter how much he practised, there was probably as much chance of him winning the lottery as becoming a professional footballer.

"Trust me," said Mike, smiling. "You've got something special, Jamie. I've known it from the very first time I ever saw you kick a football."

Jamie nodded. When it came to football, Mike knew what he was talking about. But Pratley's prediction wasn't the only problem.

"There's something else too," said Jamie. "There's a new boy coming to our school next week. He's Brazilian and everyone's madly excited to see what he's like … how cool he's going to be … how brilliant at football… But what if he's better than me? What if they make him captain of the pupils' team? What if he takes my place altogether?"

Mike shook his head. "Hang on a minute, JJ. I think you're looking at it the wrong way. How many hours have we spent talking about Brazilian football, watching those videos of their skills on the internet, wondering where they got their touch of magic from?"

"Loads," smiled Jamie. "More than Mum likes, anyway."

"And now you've got a Brazilian boy coming to your school? You shouldn't be worried, Jamie, you should be excited! If I were you, I'd be preparing a list of questions right now. If you want to be a professional, you should be asking this boy all the secrets of Brazilian football … and make sure you tell me!"

"And, by the way," said Mike, suddenly getting quite excited, "if he is half as good as you, you two could develop a partnership and play upfront for Hawkstone one day. What did you say his name was again?"

"Rafael da Cruz," said Jamie.

"Yes," said Mike, warming further to the idea. "I like

that. Johnson and da Cruz, the Brit and the Brazilian, the deadly striking duo to fire Hawkstone United to league title…"

As Mike leaned back and conjured the image of his grandson inspiring his beloved Hawkstone United to lift the league title, Jamie shifted uneasily in his chair.

All of Mike's words hadn't yet convinced him that Pratley was wrong. And his hopes of captaining the pupils' football team were under grave threat too. He had learned that, in football, there was usually only room for one real star in any team… And Jamie knew that, just about now, flying across the sky was a player from Brazil who might have the talent to outshine him completely.

6

Cruz Control

Monday 5 May

"How many kick-ups can you do?" the boy demanded, arrogance oozing from every pore.

"I don't know," said Jamie. "Maybe fifty or sixty…"

"Ha!" said the boy. "My record is four hundred and sixty-eight."

Right there and then, in the school hall, the boy started doing kick-ups and before long, the whole school was watching and cheering.

"You're amazing! How do you do it?" all the kids asked, wowed by the boy's ability.

"Ha!" smiled the boy, flicking back his long black hair while continuing his kick-ups. "I have complete mastery of the football. I can even do kick-ups with my eyes shut – watch! My name is Rafael da Cruz. I am Brazilian. This is what I do."

When he had finished showing off his tricks and skills, all the girls queued up to hug him. Jack even kissed him on the cheek and, while she did so, the boy just stared right at Jamie with a self-important smile.

"We are honoured to have a Brazilian at our school!" said Mr Karenza, joining the queue to speak to the new arrival. "And I know the Year 6 kids have already decided that they would like you to be the captain in our big football match at the end of the year. Everyone has seen your skills. We all know you're a way better player than Jamie Johnson."

Jamie woke up in a dark mood. He could feel his anger spitting inside him like a volcano just before it is about to erupt.

He had hardly slept all night and, when he had, his dreams had been filled with horrible visions of this boy from Brazil suddenly arriving at Wheatlands and snatching control of the whole school.

The thought of losing his position as the best player in the year and perhaps even his friendship with Jack too made Jamie feel sick.

He smashed open his boiled egg and ground his

teeth together as, without warning, his mind once again visualized the image of the cool Brazilian striding into school.

"I'll pick you up from Mike's at around eight o'clock tonight, got another double shif—" Jamie's mum was in the middle of saying as he slammed the front door shut behind him and stomped up the road to school.

Jamie already knew that this anger would be with him all day. His moods were like heavy cloaks, almost impossible to shake off. The truth was, he hated this Brazilian boy before he had even met him.

At approximately 1.10 that afternoon, a very strangely dressed boy walked into the Wheatlands school hall during lunch.

The boy was covered from head to toe in a huge beige anorak. The hood was over his head so far that his face was barely visible and the sleeves were stretched to cover his hands.

Without looking a single person in the eye or speaking to a soul, he sat down on a table all by himself and began to slowly eat a packed lunch.

All the children stared at him and a couple even introduced themselves and tried to start a conversation, but the boy still refused to say a word or make eye contact.

Fevered speculation began to mount. Was that him? Could it really be him?

None of the kids could believe it until, sure enough, just before the end of lunch, Mr Karenza entered the hall to make a short announcement.

"Everyone," he smiled. "This is Rafael da Cruz. Please make him feel very welcome."

7

Pratley's Plan

"Right, boys," said Mr Pratley as the last of the lunch benches were removed from the school hall. "We're going to play football today."

His announcement was met with complete and utter shock.

The boys and girls were separated for PE. This year, the girls got to go outside in the playground with the new teacher, Ms Vetterlein, who allowed them to play football every week. Jack always raved about the quality of the sessions. Not only was Ms Vetterlein an awesome striker herself and an actual member of the Hawkstone United Women's Team, she also coached all the girls to become better players themselves. The only problem, Jack admitted, was that playing against Ms Vetterlein in the Teachers v Pupils game was going to be an absolute nightmare!

Meanwhile, the boys had to be inside with Mr Pratley, who had never let them play football even once. Yet today, for some reason, not only were they playing – but it was Pratley's suggestion.

Almost everyone cheered when he made his announcement.

The one person who did not cheer, however, was Jamie. There was something about this that he didn't like. Something that gave him a weird feeling. *Why today?* Jamie asked himself. *Why is he letting us play football today?*

"OK!" said Pratley with a worryingly large smile. "Johnson, you can be one captain and ... let me see ... yes, da Cruz ... you can be the other."

"OOOOOOhhhh!" was the collective response from the rest of the players, who, as one, immediately understood the gravity of what was about to happen.

This was it ... straight away! Within just a couple of hours of Rafael da Cruz joining school, he was already going to be playing football against Jamie Johnson. A match-up between the best player in the school and the new boy from Brazil. People had been talking about this moment ever since they knew Rafael would be joining the school and now it was here. Already.

And it was perfect timing too; all of this week, the Year 6s would be secretly voting for who their captain would be in the Teachers v Pupils match. This contest would undoubtedly show everyone who was the greatest footballer in Year 6.

For the first time, Jamie looked at the Brazilian boy properly. He took in his features: his short black curly hair, his dark, tanned skin ... the contrast to Jamie's straight red hair and pale white skin could not have been more marked.

Glaring at his rival, Jamie felt his heart start to pump. A single bead of sweat began to trickle down his forehead. Then, as he watched Pratley pick the two teams, he felt a horror spread throughout him. The teams were wildly, outrageously unfair.

"What?" said Kai Thomas to Jamie, as the two team line-ups were completed. "They've got Aaron ... and Dexter ... and Kane ... AND the Brazilian! That's way unfair! We're going to get BATTERED!"

"Let's see what happens," responded Jamie. Outwardly, he was trying to appear calm. That was his responsibility as a captain. Inside, he was distraught. Now he understood exactly why Pratley was letting them play football; this whole game was designed to show Jamie up and make the Brazilian look great.

Pratley was trying to destroy Jamie's football reputation.

8
"Tackle Him!"

Jamie wished that Jack was with him. It was stupid that they split the boys and girls up for PE. She loved football as much as anyone and she was one of the best players too. If she was on Jamie's team now, he knew they could still win – even against the Brazilian.

It was as that thought crossed his mind that Jamie realized the Brazilian had been incredibly quiet during all of the pre-match commotion. Indeed, Jamie had not even heard the boy talk yet.

Jamie looked over and saw that, since Pratley had announced the playing of this match, the Brazilian boy had not moved an inch. He was still standing in exactly the same place: right in the middle of the hall, clutching on to what looked like some kind of notepad.

"Go on, da Cruz, get back into your own half," ordered Pratley. "We're going to kick off now. Perhaps you might demonstrate to Johnson that there is more to the game of football than just running fast!"

Pratley started laughing again. Jamie felt his anger rising.

Yet the boy still remained exactly where he was. Was he in some kind of trance? Did he even understand English?

"Well come on then!" Pratley barked at the boy. "What are you waiting for?"

The boy frowned and shook his head.

"Get into your position!" yelled Pratley. "Let's see what you can do!"

And with that, Pratley blew his whistle and tossed the ball high into the air.

As the ball spiralled upwards, Jamie instantly felt the electricity shoot through his body. He felt the same powerful sensation when he started playing any game of football.

"It's called an adrenaline buzz," Mike had told him. "You get it if you're scared, angry or excited. It's your brain giving your body extra power to do what it needs to do."

Jamie knew his brain was right. It was time for him to do what he had to do.

"Yes, Kai!" called Jamie, immediately from the kick-off. "Go on, pass it!"

Jamie was already marked by Aaron Cody, one of the best players on the other side, but both Kai and Jamie knew one thing: their team's best and only tactic was to get Jamie the ball as quickly as possible.

Kai chipped the ball to Jamie, who, feeling Aaron close behind him, turned him in one swift move … and now he was on the run.

Pushing the ball forward, Jamie raced like lightning down the hall, the other players fading away from him as he produced a run of breathtaking pace.

Within three seconds, Jamie's pure velocity had taken him from one end of the hall to the other and now, out of the corner of his eye, he registered that the biggest test was about to come. There was just one player left between him and the goalkeeper.

The Brazilian.

Jamie knew he had to get this absolutely right. He didn't have many tricks, so he would have to beat the Brazilian with his speed.

Jamie brought the ball to a complete stop – to make

sure the Brazilian was flat on his feet – before firing away from him again like a bullet.

Taking extra-special care to place his shot into the corner, Jamie swept the ball home to put his side 1–0 up.

"Beauty!" he roared, running to pick the ball out of the net before racing back to his own half, giving all of his jubilant teammates a high five on the way. He made sure to give the Brazilian and everyone else on the pitch a stare. A stare that said the other side had *some* of the best players … but they didn't have Jamie.

As Jamie ran past the Brazilian, he realized that the boy hadn't actually tried to tackle him; he'd just let Jamie get through. Even now, he still hadn't really moved. For some strange reason, he seemed more interested in holding on to that little notepad that he was carrying.

The game kicked off again straight away and immediately swung back the other way. Stung into action by Jamie's strike, Dexter and Kane Talbot, two skilful twins (one left footed, one right) combined to play a series of telepathic one twos to rip right through the heart of Jamie's team. They even passed the ball to each other on the goal line before Dexter finished off the classic move to level the game up at 1–1.

Yet, even as their whole team was celebrating, Jamie

noticed that the Brazilian was not involved in the action in any way. Instead, he had opened his little notepad, taken a pencil from his pocket, and was writing something down. In the middle of the game!

"Put that notepad away now!" shouted Pratley.

Hearing Pratley's yell, Rafael da Cruz reluctantly put the notepad back in his pocket. It was impossible not to notice that he had started to look very sad.

Jamie was utterly confused. Rafael was so different to the Brazilian boy that everyone had been expecting.

Perhaps, though, he was just a slow starter. Perhaps he needed to get used to his new surroundings before he felt comfortable enough to play. Or perhaps he was being sneaky, fooling the other players by pretending that he was no good, getting ready to take everyone by surprise and stun them with his talent.

Jamie had to know the truth. He had to know how good this boy really was. There was only one way find out. Jamie had to take on Rafael again.

As soon as he next received the ball, Jamie rampaged through the centre of the opposing team's defence. Again, he used no skills, just his raw, unmatchable pace. Almost inevitably, it resulted in the same situation: Jamie coming one on one with Rafael.

Let's see how you handle this one, he thought as he kicked the ball to one side of Rafael and scampered around the other to collect it. It was a simple but great move – one of Jamie's favourites.

Jamie was just sprinting past Rafael when the entire hall was suddenly filled with the tumultuous sound of pure anger.

"For GOD'S SAKE ... TACKLE HIM!!!!" exploded Pratley. Stung into action by fear, Rafael turned and launched his body into Jamie's. The contact was immediate. Both players clattered into each other, tumbling over in a tangle of flying limbs. The screeching sound of skin burning on the hall floor told everyone that this was serious.

Jamie came to a halt and immediately looked at his bare arm. It was completely covered in a friction burn, which was sending a violent pain through him.

"What did you do that for?" Jamie snarled. "You knew I'd beaten you but you still took me down, you dirty fouler!"

"S-s-sorry," said Rafael, trying to get to his feet.

"So you should be!" shouted Jamie, converting all of his frustration into one powerful push to shove Rafael back down to the ground.

9

Thousands of Miles From Home

"I can't tell you how disappointed I am by all of this. I really am," the head teacher, Mr Karenza, said gravely, leaning back in his chair, looking at the two offenders.

This was the first time in months that Jamie had been sent to the head's office and he hated being here. Mr Pratley could shout as loudly as he wanted and it never scared Jamie – if anything, he just found it funny. However, with Mr Karenza it was the complete opposite: he had only lost his temper once in all the time Jamie had been at the school, but Jamie could still remember it. He shuddered at the thought.

"Jamie, I would never have expected this of you. I

thought you would have been one of the people to have made Rafael most welcome in our school," Mr Karenza said.

"Can you imagine how difficult it must be to arrive in a new country thousands of miles from your home? What do you think your mother would make of this if I told her?"

Jamie shook his head and looked at the floor.

"And Rafael, to get into a fight on your first day … within hours of arriving! After everything your father has done to get you into this school…"

Mr Karenza took off his glasses and rubbed his eyes. "And Mr Pratley tells me that you pretty much refused to play football? Why was that, Rafael? Your dad told me you love football."

"I d-d-d-do love football," Rafael stammered.

Jamie stared at him. He realized it was the first time he had heard Rafael say a whole sentence. Or rather, try to.

"B-b-b-b-ut I d-d-don't play. I l-l-love it in a d-d-d-different way."

As he attempted to speak, each letter and syllable seemed to be like a dagger in his throat. The more he tried to get the words out of his mouth, the harder and more painfully they seemed to stay blocked inside him.

Jamie was shocked, and he immediately understood

why Rafael had not wanted to speak earlier. He really felt for him.

"Fine," said Mr Karenza, also a little more sensitively. He was making notes on a piece of paper as he spoke.

"Well, we don't force anyone into anything here at Wheatlands so, in future, you certainly don't have to play football if you don't want to. However, we cannot allow the fighting to go unpunished, so the two of you will help the dinner ladies clean up the hall after lunch every day for the rest of the week, and if I ever hear about either of you fighting again, believe me, the consequences will be far, far worse. Is that clear?"

Both boys nodded and, as they did so, Jamie attempted to offer the smallest of smiles in Rafael's direction.

"What was all that about?" asked Jack as soon as Jamie and Rafael came out of Mr Karenza's office.

"Fighting," Jamie said, watching Rafael walk away. "He's the one who started it ... but I don't think it was really his fault."

"You and your temper," said Jack. "I feel sorry for whoever has to be your manager in the future."

But Jamie wasn't listening. He was watching Rafael slope away down the corridor by himself.

There was something that Mr Karenza had said

which made sense. When he'd asked Jamie how he'd have felt if *he* were the one joining a new school thousands of miles from home, one single word had immediately inserted itself into Jamie's head.

It was the same word that described how Rafael da Cruz had looked since the moment he had arrived at Wheatlands:

Lost.

⑩
Pollock's Delight

Friday 9 May – four days later

Jamie stared at the baked beans splattered across the table. The red, gooey liquid was dripping off the edge and trickling down on to the bench below.

He took a deep breath, held his nose and wiped it clean.

Cleaning out the hall after lunch was by far the worst punishment that the school handed out, and Jamie felt sure that Pratley had specifically requested it when he had sent the two boys to Mr Karenza for their fight. Certainly, Pratley had been watching them both with eagle eyes every day this week as they carried out their humiliating duties.

Yesterday, Pratley had even come up to Jamie and said smugly: "Learning your lesson, Johnson?" as Jamie had been emptying out the stinking rubbish bin.

Still, at least now it was the end of the week and this would be the last day of the torture. Not that Jamie's plight was anything as bad as Rafael's; Jamie only had to clean up the mess. Rafael also had to put up with the teasing … and today it seemed to be getting even worse.

"Oh no, I've spilled my spaghetti on the floor!" said Edgar Pollock, the most annoying boy in Year 5. He thought that just because he was really rich, he could order other people around. Worse still were the kids who hung around with him just because he had money.

"Will you come and p-p-p-pick it up for me, Rafael?" Edgar and his friends erupted into raucous laughter and watched with delight as Rafael bent down and cleared up all the mess. However, just as Rafael had finished, Pollock purposely tipped the rest of his plate over too.

"Oh no! Look what I've done now!" he cackled. "So sorry, R-R-R-Rafael!"

Jamie shook his head. Word had now gone round and some of the kids had started to talk about the fact that Rafael had a stutter. If someone had done to Jamie what Edgar had just done to Rafael, Jamie would have lost his cool and lashed out.

Yet as he watched Rafael slowly complete his dreadful, degrading cleaning mission, Jamie was struck by the fact that he neither reacted nor showed he was affected.

There was no doubt that there was something very different about this boy. Jamie just couldn't work out whether that was a good thing or a bad thing.

⑪
Noted

"He's not what I was expecting – I know that for sure," said Jamie as he and Jack walked home, passing a stone between them. "I think I like him but it's, you know, difficult to get close to him. And what's the thing with his notepad? Why's he always carrying it around?"

"Exactly," agreed Jack, flicking the stone into the air and volleying it further down the street to allow them to quicken their pace. "And that's not all. Have you seen him when we're playing football in the playground?"

Jamie shook his head.

"Just have a look on Monday," she smiled. "See what you make of it."

Saturday 10 May

This was Jamie's favourite bit.

Giving the ticket collector his season ticket, seeing them check it and then release the catch for Jamie to be able to push his way into the stadium. Into the home of Hawkstone United.

He could easily have run up all eighty-seven steps to get to their seats, but he knew that Mike couldn't run any more, so they climbed the steps together. It made Jamie sad to think Mike walked with a limp. And sadder still to think that the brilliant career he would have had as a Hawkstone player was stolen away from him at such a young age by his horrific knee injury. But as they slowly climbed the stairs, Jamie felt proud and excited to be with a man who he admired so much. That was the point of being here at Hawkstone. It wasn't just the football. It was being together.

They always arrived half an hour before the kick-off in order to see the whole of the warm-up. Jamie loved watching the strikers pinging the balls into the top corner of the net from all types of outrageous angles. He could never understand why most of the fans stood outside the ground drinking and eating right until the last minute before they came in.

They were missing some of the best stuff. This was

the chance to see how good these top performers really were.

"Mike, can I ask you something?" said Jamie as the players jogged down the tunnel to receive their final instructions before the kick-off.

This was the last game of the season. Jamie and Mike had not missed a single home match for three years. No matter how well or badly Hawkstone did, Jamie would always support them for the rest of his life. They were part of who he was.

"Sure," said Mike, rising from his seat to stand up. He always did this just before the game started. It was his knee; if he sat down for too long without getting up, the knee locked and gave him excruciating pain.

"Was there ever any bullying when you went to school?" asked Jamie.

Mike's face changed and hardened.

"Is someone being mean to you about your dad again, JJ?" he demanded. "Tell me who it is and I'll sort them out. They'll be sorry they ever—"

"No, Mike, it's not me, don't worry," laughed Jamie. "It's someone else. That Brazilian kid I was telling you about before. He's arrived now and he's ... kind of different. Different to how we thought he was going to be, anyway, and some of the other kids are just giving him a bit of a hard time."

"Oh," said Mike, straightening his coat and peering towards the tunnel. The players were beginning to assemble now. It was nearly time. "Well, you know that just because other kids are giving him a hard time doesn't mean that you have to."

Jamie nodded. But he also knew it wasn't as easy as that.

"I've never understood why people think being different is a bad thing," said Mike, putting his arm around Jamie's shoulder. Jamie knew that in a minute Mike would start the singing and the chanting. He'd once been the captain of the Hawkstone Youth Team. Now, he was the leader of the Hawkstone fans.

"Kids can be cruel," said Mike. "It comes from fear. They're scared of the other kids thinking they're not cool. What they don't understand is that real coolness is having the guts to go your own way – to be who *you* are.

"And anyway," he smiled. "Who wants to be exactly the same as everyone else? To me, that sounds seriously boring!"

Then Mike gave Jamie the nod. They both knew what it meant.

It was time to start shouting for Hawkstone at the very top of their voices.

"Get the Notepad!"

Monday 12 May

"How long's he been there?" grinned Jamie.

It had been a good morning. No, it had been a great morning.

In assembly, it had been announced that Jamie Johnson had won the vote by what Mr Karenza had described as a "very clear majority". Jamie was to be captain of the Pupils Team.

With the whole school watching, Jamie had walked to the front, where he and Pratley, as the two captains, had been made to shake hands and pretend they were best friends.

Jamie had thought about tickling the inside

of Pratley's palm as they shook hands but decided against it at the last minute. *Always stand up for yourself,* Mike told him, *but never wind up your opponent – it only gives them an extra incentive to beat you.*

"He's been there every second of every match we've played since he arrived," said Jack, answering Jamie's earlier question and snapping him back into the break-time game they were playing.

Jamie looked to see that Rafael was crouching down, behind one of the goals on the playground, almost entirely hidden by a car.

Squatting down like that, he seemed as though he were on some kind of police stake-out or attempting to catch a glimpse of a leopard in the wild. He looked weird.

"Seriously?" said Jamie. "He's watched all our games at break like that? And he's still writing in that notepad! What is he putting in there?"

Jamie was intrigued. But there was no time to think about Rafael right now. There was a game going on and every day counted. Literally. Last night Jamie had calculated that there were only forty-three more school days until the Pupils v Teachers game.

People were relying on him to make history. He had to be ready.

"Yes!" Jamie shouted as Jack leapt high to snatch a ball out of the air.

She looked up and saw that Jamie was tightly marked, but she also knew that she could still pass to him; he'd have the pace to get away. In a whir of motion, she spun the ball out to Jamie, who was waiting to collect it on the left wing.

Jamie stretched out his foot to accept the ball softly and bring it under his control. *Use your feet like hands*, Mike had told him once, as he showed Jamie how to kill the ball dead in an instant. He may not have been able to run any more, but Mike still had the touch of a professional.

As soon as the ball was with him, the football computer in Jamie's head kicked in. It calculated the distance between him and the goal and instantly worked out the rate at which he needed to run.

Then Jamie clicked into his turbo gear, burning past two defenders in a flash of Olympic speed. The ball was tied to his foot as he surged ahead of the opposition in a blur of blistering pace.

In his head, Jamie could hear the commentator shouting, ever more excitedly:

Johnson ... still Johnson ... still Johnson ... STILL Johnson... He's going to SHOOT!

As Jamie drew back his left leg, everyone in the

playground stopped to watch. The sun shone down from above the school building, illuminating the image of Jamie's body, perfectly shaped, ready to exert maximum power. Then Jamie brought his foot towards the ball with breathtaking speed.

He struck the ball so perfectly, so fully, so sweetly that it immediately began whistling through the air towards the goal. Jamie was just about to wheel away in celebration when he saw that his strike had actually not hit the net but instead had thundered into the angle of post and crossbar. It rebounded off the metal frame of the goal and was now ricocheting straight towards Rafael.

There was not even time for Rafael to move. The ball was going far too fast.

"Ooooh!"

There was a gasp from everyone on the playground as the ball smashed brutally into the middle of Rafael's face, knocking him clean off his feet. As he fell backwards, hitting his head against the side of the car, his notepad went flying into the air.

"Get the notepad!" one of the kids shouted as they realized that this was their opportunity to grab the boy's most precious item. Hearing their plan, Rafael tried to scramble to his feet, but it was no use – he had hit his head so hard he barely knew where he was.

Jamie stood and watched. He saw the other boys charging towards Rafael, determined to steal his notepad. He saw Rafael, with a tear nestling in his eye, desperately trying to stop them … and something inside Jamie clicked.

It was almost the same feeling as when the anger rushed upon him…

Jamie had been teased before: for having red hair, for being thin and small and pale. And the cruellest taunts of all had come when his dad had left.

No, Jamie didn't feel anger towards Rafael. He wanted to help.

Jamie's eyes zoomed in on Rafael's location before scanning the area around him. Immediately, he detected where the notepad had landed.

The other kids were all looking next to Rafael, but the notepad had actually landed on the other side of the car, by the wheel. It must have looped up and over the vehicle when Rafael had been thrown backwards by the power of Jamie's shot.

Jamie still had no idea what was so special about this notepad but he also knew that that didn't matter. It belonged to Rafael. That was what was important.

The computer in Jamie's head kicked back in,

analysing the distance he was from the notepad ... but now the other kids had seen it too. It was a straight race between them and Jamie.

Jamie Johnson didn't lose races.

He dashed across the playground and rolled under the car, scooping up the notepad just in time.

Then Jamie stood up as tall as he could and, with all the kids on the playground looking at him, he spoke with his loudest possible voice.

"Let's ... just ... give Rafael a break," he said.

As the final word escaped from his mouth, Jamie realized how fast his heart was pumping. For a second, he just stood there panting.

Then he walked slowly over to Rafael and, resisting the temptation to look inside, placed the notepad back into his palm.

"How about you and me start again?" said Jamie, stretching out his hand.

Rafael looked down at the notepad before breathing what looked like a long sigh of relief.

Then he stared at Jamie's outstretched hand. The expression on Rafael's face was like that of a starving wild animal being offered food by a stranger: wanting to accept it but fearing it might be a trap.

Jamie gave Rafael his biggest smile. He meant the boy no harm.

Then, for the first time, Rafael smiled back. A big, warm Brazilian smile.

"*O-o-o-brigado*, J-Jamie," said Rafael, shaking Jamie's right hand while clutching his notepad to his chest with the other.

Jamie looked at Rafael, slightly confused.

"Thank you?" he guessed.

Rafael nodded.

"Th-th-ank y-you."

(13)

"You Must Be a Genius!"

Friday 23 May –
eleven days later

"Championes, championes olé, olé, olé!
Championes, championes olé, olé, olé!"

Hawkstone United, jointly managed by Jamie Johnson and Rafael da Cruz, were the Champions of Europe! With brave attack-minded tactics, they had beaten every other team on the continent. They were the kings of Soccer Manager!

"Shall we start a new one?" suggested Jamie as soon as they had finished celebrating.

That was the thing about this computer game: the more they played, the more addicted they became.

"Load it up!" responded Rafael. "But this time I want us to try a new formation."

The seeds of the partnership had been sown in that moment when Jamie stood up for Rafael in the playground.

Jack had then suggested that Rafael sit with her and Jamie at lunch, and quickly he became a fixture alongside them in lessons too. Initially some of the other kids gave Jamie strange looks, as if to say, *Why are you being so nice to the weird kid?* But Jamie didn't care. He liked Rafael. And who wanted to be normal anyway?

Then, one day, in the middle of a maths lesson, when Pratley had his back turned, Rafael had nudged Jamie mischievously and torn a sheet out of his notepad, handing it to Jamie with a cheeky wink.

On the page was a drawing of Pratley with his eyes popping out and a bogey coming from his nose, wagging his finger at Jamie, telling him off. At the top was written "Pratley vs Jamie", and at the bottom Rafael had written, "Is this right, Jamie?"

As well as being amazed by Rafael's artistic talent, Jamie had got the most intense giggles and been sent out straight away … but he took the drawing with him.

Jamie didn't want Pratley to find out what he was

Pratley Vs Jamie

Is this right, Jamie?

laughing at and for Rafael to get into trouble too. Besides, he wanted to put that drawing up on his bedroom wall!

That incident seemed to make Rafael trust Jamie even more and when, that same afternoon, Jamie had invited him back to his house for the first time, Rafael accepted.

Swiftly and naturally, they had slipped into their routine: each day, Jamie, Jack and Rafael walked to the park after school, where Jamie took shots at Jack while Rafael looked on and made notes in his pad. Then they walked on to Jack's house and dropped her home before Jamie and Rafael would play Soccer Manager for hours and hours in Jamie's room, stopping only to go to the toilet or to eat some toast. Their marathon sessions lasted until Rafael's dad, Bernard, came to pick him up in the evening. It worked perfectly for everyone because Bernard, who was an architect working on Hawkstone's brand-new shopping centre, was always at the office until late anyway.

When Bernard arrived – generally in a suit and always looking serious but cool – Jamie and Rafael would simply pause the game and carry on the next day.

It was while they were playing Soccer Manager five days before that something quite amazing had happened. During a toast break, Jamie asked Rafael to talk again about what football was really like in Brazil. He asked Rafael the same question every day. Jamie was so fascinated by Brazilian football, he couldn't stop thinking about it. What he really wanted to know was what made the Brazilian footballers so unique. What gave them the bit of magic in their play that no one else in the world possessed?

Rafael was always happy to talk about Brazilian football, but what had been different about that day was the way in which he had answered the question ... the way he had spoken.

"Football in Brazil is our life, our religion ... it is everything," Rafael had smiled. "Every person in the country is in love with football... Me, for example, my dad took me to watch Palmeiras, his favourite team, when I was a baby! We go to watch them all the time and every game is like a party. The fans, they go to dance and sing. It is such a beautiful experience. Oh, and by the way, Palmeiras have a new young player. He is an attacker called Arnaldo and he has the most brilliant skills. He has the magic in his play that you are talking about. Believe me, everyone in the world will soon have heard of him."

It was only when Rafael paused for breath that they both stopped and looked at each other. Rafael had not stammered once the whole time he had been talking.

"Rafael!" Jamie beamed. "What just happened?!"

"I don't know..." grinned Rafael, exploring his new-found ability. "I spoke without a stutter ... I still am!"

It had continued in the same way for the whole afternoon and evening, but as soon as they were back at school, Rafael's stutter had returned. And Rafael had confided that it was still there when he was at home with his dad too. And yet these days, when it was just him and Jamie, chilling in Jamie's room, there was no sign of the stutter whatsoever. It was a kind of little miracle that neither of them talked too much about, just in case it went away again.

"OK, we'll play as Palmeiras this time, and I want to try to play a 3-3-2-2 formation," said Rafael as Jamie loaded up a new game. They had been playing for four hours straight as Hawkstone United and had already conquered Europe in the last game but they still wanted more. Now, as a Brazilian team, they wanted to take on the world!

The pair managing Palmeiras was also part of an important deal that the two boys had struck between them: Rafael had agreed that, from now on, Hawkstone United would be his team to support in the Premier League. In return, Jamie would now follow Palmeiras as his favourite foreign team. It meant exchanging lots of information about the clubs and players of the past and it also meant playing twice as many games on Soccer Manager to ensure that both Hawkstone and Palmeiras got their fair share of success. But that was fine, especially as the half-term holiday was just about to begin!

"Playing 3-3-2-2 is an experiment but I think it can work," Rafael explained, outlining his vision further. "We'll have three defenders at the back to deal with the one striker that most teams go with, a bank of three in front to look after the forward runs of the opposition midfield, two creative central midfielders to cause problems between the lines … and two attackers – but not central ones. I want them to play out wide, to stop the opposing full-backs and, of course, also to cut in for lots of shots themselves. I want it to rain goals!"

Jamie did not respond. How could he? Just as Jamie's brain could analyse and calculate speeds and angles on the football pitch, Rafael's seemed to be able to retain all of the information off the football pitch. His powers of recall were phenomenal. It was as if he had a football version of a photographic memory.

"What do think?" smiled Rafael.

"I think you must be a genius!" said Jamie.

He was still staring at Rafael, in awe of his friend's vast football knowledge, when the doorbell went.

14

Private Conversation

"You go and wait in the car, Rafa," said Bernard. "I want to speak to Jamie's mother for a minute."

Rafael looked at his dad and nodded. Then he gave Jamie a quick high five and a big smile.

"Go on," Bernard repeated. "I'll be there in five minutes."

"See y-y-ou s-o-on," said Rafael.

"Cool," said Jamie, realizing Rafael's stutter had returned as soon as it wasn't just the two of them any more. "Why don't you come over next week so we can start another game with your new tactics?"

Rafael didn't respond to Jamie's invitation. He simply smiled again – almost as though he knew something that Jamie didn't – and then left the house, closing the door behind him.

For a second, there was silence, both Jamie and his mum staring at Bernard, wondering what he wanted.

"Would it be OK if I spoke to your mum alone for a bit?" Bernard asked. He looked so serious, Jamie wondered if something really bad had happened, but that was how Rafael's dad always looked: cool but seriously serious.

Jamie walked up the stairs, opened the door to his bedroom and then shut it loudly ... but he didn't go inside. The noise was just to make sure that Bernard and his mum thought he was in his room. There was no way he was going to miss this.

Jamie crouched down and, very slowly, so as not to make even the tiniest creak in the floorboards, crawled to the top of the stairs, where he would be able to hear what they were saying without them being able to see him.

"...I know it would make Rafael extremely happy and me too," Bernard was saying. Jamie could hear the kettle boiling. His mum always put on the kettle when she talked to people in the kitchen.

"Milk? Sugar?" she asked.

"No, just black is great, thank you," said Bernard.

"So, what do you think, Karen? We think Jamie would love Brazil and it would be our absolute pleasure to have him with us."

Jamie's whole body froze rigid. Had he just heard what he thought he'd heard?

"There you go," she said, her voice completely calm. "Listen, Bernard, it really is very kind of you to make such an offer and I've no doubt that Jamie would absolutely love to go to Rio with you but ... well, there's no way we can accept, I'm afraid."

"I see..." said Bernard.

At the top of the stairs, Jamie was beginning to shake. This was too big ... surely she couldn't be saying no. *Why*? he silently mouthed in anguish.

"And why is that?" asked Bernard.

"Where do I start?" said his mum. "Jamie's never even been out of this country before – Brazil is practically the other side of the world. The longest he's ever spent away from home is two nights on a school trip, now suddenly we're talking about a whole week ... not to mention the fact that there's absolutely no way on earth that we can afford it."

Jamie clenched his fist and bit it as hard as he could. Going to Brazil would be, without doubt, the most exciting thing he could do in his life ... and yet his mum was saying there was "no way on earth" it was going to happen. All he wanted to do was scream.

"Maybe if you could wait until the summer holidays … then the boys will know each other a bit better and we'll all have time to prepare for it rather than just … springing it on us the night before."

"I do realize this is last minute," acknowledged Bernard. "It's just that Rafael and I have to go back this week – we fly in the morning. There is something we have to be there for, that can't be changed.

"We only had the idea last night. Rafael was telling me how much he likes Jamie and how kind Jamie has been to him and we just thought it would be a nice idea … make it a really nice half-term for him. We are sure Jamie would love Brazil.

"And, please," he continued. "Don't worry about the cost. It would be my pleasure to pay for Jamie's ticket. It's the least I can do. So just let me know if you change your mind."

15
Help!

Jamie waited until he heard Bernard's BMW start up and drive off. Then he sprinted down the stairs and unleashed his venom.

"Why did you do that?!" he screamed at his mum. His face was bright red with fury.

"Jamie! You were listening? You shouldn't have been listen—"

"Do you have any idea how much this would mean to me? To go to Brazil with Rafael, to see them play football over there ... to learn from them? I'll never get a chance like this again in my life and you're ruining it! Do you want me to hate you?!"

"Jamie! Do NOT talk to me like that! I'm not doing this to be cruel to you. I'm trying to do what's right. It's all way too quick to make such a big decision."

Jamie had already slammed the door behind him. He was running. Sprinting as hard as he could, hammering out the frustration and anger through his legs on to the pavement. He was tearing through the streets, his body charged with rage.

If he knew where his dad was now, he would run to him and beg him to let him live there ... but he couldn't do that. There was only one place left to run.

"You should never say you hate anyone, JJ. Least of all your mum," said Mike, once Jamie had got it all out. For the first few minutes after he'd arrived he had been so upset he hadn't even been able to talk.

"You need to apologize," said Mike, walking into the kitchen. "I'm up for toasted cheese. You?"

"No way!" snapped Jamie, ignoring Mike's offer. "Why should *I* apologize? She should be the one saying sorry to me! She's the one stopping me from doing the most amazing thing I'm ever going to do in my life! What's wrong with her?"

Jamie's whole body was a cauldron of boiling resentment. Why didn't she just concentrate on her own life instead of ruining his?

"She's not some cruel dictator," said Mike, slipping

a bit of cheese into his mouth as he prepared his sandwich. "She's your mum."

Jamie got up and smashed Mike's tennis ball against the wall. He couldn't sit still.

"Just do something, Mike," said Jamie, trying to hit the ball again, even harder this time. But he swung his foot at the ball so violently he missed it altogether. This wasn't the first time this had happened; when he argued with his mum, his football was always the first thing to suffer, which only made him even more frustrated.

"Make her understand what this means. This is Brazil! Aren't you the one who said I should be asking Rafael everything about football over there? Well, this is my chance to actually go. Don't you always tell me never to give up on my dreams? This *is* my dream! You know that! You've got to stop her, Mike! Please!! Before it's too late!"

Mike took a firm grip of his grandson and held him in a cool stare.

"Jamie," he said, with a strong, even voice. "Everything that you have in this world, including your existence, is because of that woman. Remember that. Now, do you want my help or not?"

16

Language of Football

Jamie and his mum had both been going mad, for different reasons. His mum knew she couldn't be late for her shift at the hospital for the second time this week and Jamie was beyond desperate to know what Mike and Bernard had been talking about for this long.

Once Jamie had calmed down (having eaten two of Mike's jumbo-sized toasted cheese sandwiches) they had both gone back to Jamie's house and Jamie had finally apologized for losing his temper. Then Mike had suggested that perhaps he should just go and have a chat with Bernard, if only to get a bit more information. What harm could it do?

Jamie had given Mike the address and Mike headed off straight away. But that had been two and a half hours ago. Since then, they had heard nothing.

When Karen and Jamie finally spotted Mike walking back up the street, they could both tell from the look on his face that something was up. He was in a world of his own. He even stopped to sit on a bench outside for a couple of minutes, looking up at the sky.

"Sit down," he'd said to both of them when he finally came in. "There's quite a lot to tell you."

Mike looked at Jamie for a second with such kind eyes that it made Jamie feel warm inside. Then his granddad started to speak.

"Rafael's mum died two years ago," he began. "Her name was Stephania and she had been ill for a very long time. It must have been … awful for them all, and since the day that she passed away, that exact day, Rafael has suffered from the most terrible stammer.

"They can't find a cure. The doctors have told Bernard that the only way Rafael will get over it is by feeling comfortable and happy again. That's the reason that Bernard brought Rafael over here: to give him a change of surroundings... To try to make him happy again. And to maybe find one person who Rafael can trust. And it seems that that person is Jamie. JJ, you never told us that Rafael doesn't stutter when it's just you and him."

Jamie nodded.

"Anyway, this is exactly what Bernard was hoping for. He called the doctors this morning and they told him that it made sense. That trust and friendship and feeling comfortable are all elements that would help Rafael find his voice again.

"Bernard believes that it's about the football too. He's got this theory that when Jamie and Rafael are talking about football, they are speaking in another language. He reckons Rafael doesn't stammer when he's talking the language of football."

Jamie nodded. Rafael was fluent in football all right.

"The last thing Bernard wants to do is split the boys up right now but he says that he and Rafael *have* to go back to Brazil for the half-term. There is an event they both need to attend. It's been planned for a long time.

"That's why he'd like Jamie to go with them. Not only do he and Rafael get to spend more time together but also as a thank-you to Jamie."

Mike paused.

"It was so difficult hearing him talk, Karen. The man looked like he hadn't smiled for such a long time."

When Mike had finished speaking, there was complete silence in the room.

"Well, I can see why you were over there for such a long time," said Jamie's mum, kissing Jamie on the forehead almost without noticing. "I had no idea that Rafael had had such a difficult time. And if Bernard thinks that Jamie being there will help Rafael speak again, then I understand a bit better why he's so keen for Jamie to go ... but it all puts a lot of pressure on Jamie, doesn't it?"

"Bernard's not expecting anything," said Mike. "He doesn't see Jamie being there as some kind of magic cure for Rafael's stutter. He just doesn't want to split the boys up at the moment. He thinks they are good for each other, so he's inviting Jamie to come along, enjoy Brazil and see what happens. He says he even knows a great coach that can teach Jamie all the Brazilian football skills."

Jamie squirmed with excitement. Ever since Pratley had told him he wouldn't make it as a professional, he'd been really depressed about his chances of fulfilling his dream. But if he could go to Brazil, if he could learn their skills, be trained in their magic, surely that would give him the extra edge so that one day he really could turn his dream into reality.

He didn't say anything. Instead, he just stared pleadingly into his mum's eyes. He had to make her understand how much he wanted this opportunity.

"I'm just ... very worried about this," said Karen. "It's so soon and, if they're going first thing in the morning, that means Jamie would have to fly by himself tomorrow night. I don't know ... I just don't know..."

Mike looked at Jamie and then he looked at Karen. His eyes seemed to sadden a little.

"Do you remember how I reacted when you had your accident?" he asked.

Karen nodded. Jamie could feel her body tighten.

Jamie knew his mum had had a bad riding accident when she was fifteen. Before that, she had been good at riding horses. Seriously good. She had been one of the best in the whole country until she had fallen one day and broken her back. Jamie knew she still kept all of her medals because he'd seen them in a special box under her bed.

"I told you that you weren't ever allowed to ride again," said Mike.

"And I ... hated you for it," said Karen. "But you were right. If I'd fallen again, anything could have happened. I could have been paralysed."

Mike shook his head. "Once you'd recovered, there was no greater risk of you falling and hurting yourself than any other rider," he said. "I just didn't want you to ride because I was scared."

Mike was twisting the ring on his finger as he spoke. Jamie could tell he was choosing his words very carefully.

"I should have listened," Mike said. "I should have understood what my child wanted from life, what her biggest dream was … and supported her every step of the way. I didn't do that for you, Karen, and I'm so sorry."

Jamie's mum started to cry, which immediately made Jamie cry too. Her being upset cut all the way through him.

"Don't be sad, Mum," Jamie said, giving her the biggest bear hug he could manage. For the first time, he realized that he got some of his sporting talent from her. "Why don't you start riding again now?"

Karen shook her head, wiped away her tears and attempted to smile.

"I just think that, if he doesn't go, Jamie will always be wondering what it would have been like," said Mike. "And believe me, life is not about wondering, it's about doing."

Karen blew her nose. She still looked unsure.

"Your boy has a dream, love," Mike said softly, smiling at Karen. "And this trip to Brazil can help him achieve it. What do you say?"

17

Not the World's Greatest Dancer

Saturday 24 May

"Just do me one favour, JJ," said Mike, looking at Jamie through the rear-view mirror. He, Jamie and Karen had been on the drive to the airport for two hours now. They had all chatted excitedly at first, followed by some time listening to music on the radio. And then it had gone quiet for a bit, until now.

"Make sure you take in every second of what you are about to experience," said Mike. "To fly to Brazil as an eleven-year-old boy... Nothing like this will ever happen to you again."

Jamie nodded. He knew.

"JJ, did I ever tell you that one of my ambitions in life

was to go to Brazil, watch a match out there and then dance all night ... you know, proper samba style?"

Jamie and Karen couldn't help but chuckle. Mike had many plus points, but he was not the world's greatest dancer.

"Just to do something spontaneous like that. That's what makes you feel alive."

"What does spontaneous mean?" asked Jamie.

"Doing something on impulse," replied Mike. "Forgetting the risks and all the reasons not to do something and just doing it anyway."

Jamie nodded. He understood. That's what the best football players did. They took a risk. They produced a skill from nowhere just at the right time.

"I haven't been spontaneous enough in my life," said Mike. "It won't happen for me now. So take it all in, JJ. Never forget how lucky you are to be able to live out a dream."

Watching Mike as he drove steadily on towards the airport, Jamie felt a familiar mixture of sadness and happiness settle upon him.

When does it become too late to make your dreams come true? he wondered.

⑱
The Book

Jamie sat down in his seat, opened his rucksack and took out the two items that Mike had given him seconds before he'd got on the plane.

The first was a brand new phone – Jamie's first ever – so that they could stay in touch at any time.

The second was a small booklet that Mike had stayed up all night writing for Jamie.

MIKE JOHNSON'S
BRILLIANT BOOK
OF BRAZILIAN
KNOWLEDGE
(MADE ESPECIALLY FOR
JAMIE ON HIS FIRST-EVER
TRIP TO BRAZIL!)

As he read the words, Jamie could imagine Mike speaking them to him. Mike had an aura about him. When he talked, people always listened.

Jamie liked to picture Mike when he was the captain of the Hawkstone United Youth Team. He could see Mike gathering his team around him in a huddle, giving them words of encouragement, making them feel as though they were the greatest team in the world and could destroy anyone that they came up against.

Even now, even after all the injuries he'd had to his knees, strength was the main characteristic that Jamie associated with Mike.

Jamie looked down at his own pale, thin arms. He hoped that when he grew up, he would take after Mike and be strong, not weak like his dad.

Jamie turned the page.

THE HISTORY OF
FOOTBALL IN BRAZIL!

Right, JJ. The story of Brazilian football, so the legend goes, begins way back in 1894 when a British boy named Charles Miller arrived in the Brazilian port of Santos! Miller was in Brazil to visit his father and had just spent time at boarding school, where he had been honing his skills at his favourite sport (guess what that was?).

He stepped off the boat with two footballs. I guess those two balls changed the history not only of Brazil but also of the whole game of football.

Apparently they have a saying in Brazil:

"Os ingleses o inventaram, os brasileiros o aperfeiçoaram."

"The English invented it, the Brazilians perfected it."

IMPORTANT FACTS ABOUT BRAZIL!!

- There is no such language as Brazilian. A lot of people think that they speak Spanish in Brazil. They are wrong! In Brazil, they actually speak a Brazilian form of Portuguese. This is because Portuguese people settled there from as early as the sixteenth century.

- Although it will be hot for you, this is not the Brazilian summer. Their summer is Jan/Feb time. Weird, eh? Imagine Christmas on the beach!

- Brazil is a huge country. And when I say that I mean MASSIVE. Both in terms of size and population, it is the fifth largest country in the world. It's nearly the same size as the whole of Europe!

- The Amazon River flows through Brazil. It is the second longest river in the world. Do you know what the longest is, JJ? (It begins with the letter "N".)

- Brazilians love nicknames, especially for their footballers! Pelé's real name is Edson Arantes do Nascimento. But Pelé just works so much better!

- In Brazil there is the most unbelievable nature. Not only are there all the beaches, but there's also the jungle! Jaguars and pumas (both big hunting cats) live there. So do poisonous frogs, massive snakes and ... piranhas. Remember I told you about them, JJ? They are the fish that have sharp teeth — they sometimes attack humans!

(Don't worry, they're in the Amazon River, which is nowhere near where you are in Rio - PHEW!)

OK, that's enough of the science bit! Now for some football facts!

- Brazil is the only country to have played in every World Cup there has ever been!

- They play football everywhere. Even in the swamplands of the Amazon!

- These are the biggest clubs in Brazil and
  the cities in which they play.

Club	City
Vitória	Salvador
Golás	Goiânia
Atlético Mineiro	Belo Horizonte
Atlético Paranaense	Curitiba
Avaí	Florianópolis
Bahia	Salvador
Botafogo	Rio de Janeiro
Ceará	Fortaleza
Corinthians	São Paulo
Coritiba	Curitiba
Cruzeiro	Belo Horizonte
Figueirense	Florianópolis
Flamengo	Rio de Janeiro
Fluminense	Rio de Janeiro
Grêmio	Porto Alegre
Internacional	Porto Alegre

Palmeiras	São Paulo
Santos	Santos
São Paulo	São Paulo
Vasco da Gama	Rio de Janeiro

- On the beach, Footvolley is the most popular game. It's the same as volleyball but you use your feet, not your hands!

- Futsal is also seriously popular. This is indoor football but with smaller goals and a smaller ball. It makes you concentrate more on skill. You know Ronaldinho grew up playing futsal — see what I mean about it improving your skills!

- Listen out for the word **caneta** when you're over there. That's what the Brazilians call a nutmeg — when you kick the ball between someone's legs. They go crazy for it over there, apparently!

This was by far the best book Jamie had ever read! The more facts that he could get about football the better! And there was still another whole chapter on the Legends of Brazilian Football to go … but the revving of the engines told Jamie that the plane was ready to take off.

He put the booklet down and looked out of the window.

He thought that his mum and Mike would probably be nearly home by now. Jamie knew how difficult his mum had found it to let him go on this trip. That was why, just before he'd got on the plane, he had turned and run back to give her one more hug.

"Thank you, Mum," he'd said. "Thank you so much for letting me go for my dream."

The engines revved once more and the aeroplane sped down the runway.

Jamie's journey was about to begin.

Part
Two

⑲
The Beach

Sunday 25 May

"Are you sure you want to wear that shirt to the beach?" asked Bernard. "It'll be hot."

Jamie took a big gulp of cereal and nodded.

At one p.m., this was a late breakfast, because it had been four in the morning by the time Rafael and Bernard had picked Jamie up from the airport and driven him back to their home.

As soon as they had turned into the road, Jamie had been impressed. They must have owned one of the nicest houses in Rio. Apparently it was only a ten-minute walk to the beach, which was lucky because that was exactly where he and Rafael were heading straight after breakfast.

Jamie had texted his mum to say he'd arrived safely just before he'd gone to sleep and then he'd spent the whole night dreaming about playing football on the beach!

Both Rafael and Bernard had promised Jamie that there was someone special he would meet today. Someone who could help him learn how to play football Brazilian style...

"I have to wear this top!" Jamie smiled, answering Bernard. He looked down at his black and white Hawkstone United shirt. "It gives me good luck and helps me to play better. You might not understand it ... it's a superstitious kind of thing."

Bernard and Rafael raised their eyebrows at each other.

"What?" asked Jamie. "Why are you looking at each other like that? Loads of footballers are superstitious."

"I know that," said Bernard. He looked serious, but then again he always looked serious. "But to say to a Brazilian football fan that they don't understand superstition is like saying to an Eskimo he doesn't understand snow. Isn't that right, Rafael?"

Rafael nodded proudly. "H-h-hundred p-p-per cent."

"Perhaps you should tell Jamie about the dog that had to wee," Bernard suggested to his son, who immediately cracked up laughing. "If he thinks *he's* superstitious, wait till he hears about Biriba!"

"Botafogo is a very famous team in this country from here in Rio," began Rafael, without a hint of a stammer as they left the house to head to the beach. It was amazing: as soon as it was just the two of them, Rafael's speech was completely uninhibited. Jamie wished Bernard could see it. He even wondered whether he should record Rafael speaking like this and play it to Bernard. That would be too risky, though; if Rafael found out, he wouldn't trust Jamie any more and, from what Jamie understood, trust was the whole reason that Rafael felt able to speak freely with Jamie in the first place.

Bernard had been right. It was boiling. Jamie could feel the sweat trickling down his forehead instantly. He looked up at the sun and his eyes were dazzled by the golden rays shining down on him. He looked around him at the busy streets, all hustle and bustle – people cleaning the cars, dusting off mats and talking to each other. That was what he noticed immediately that was different from home.

At home, people ignored each other in the street. Here, all Jamie could hear was the chatter of conversation coming from everywhere. And the colours –

everyone seemed to be wearing bright, vibrantly coloured clothes.

"...And perhaps Botafogo might be the most superstitious team in Brazil," Rafael said, continuing his story with a cheeky smile that promised something entertaining to come. "...Because I am going to tell you a true story of something that happened in the last century – in the nineteen fifties.

"So, imagine this: the reserve team of Botafogo were playing a game and they were on the attack. The striker was through; one on one with the 'keeper. He looked up and had a shot and, at that precise moment, a mongrel of a dog came running on to the pitch after the ball. It ran straight at the goalkeeper and completely put him off because he didn't know whether to look at the ball or the dog! So the ball went in the net and the referee allowed it! Goal to Botafogo! Or *goooooool!* as we say here!"

"No way!" said Jamie. "Assist to the dog!"

"You got it! The dog helped them take the lead!!" joked Rafael.

They were turning off the main road now and into some smaller side streets. There was a steep downward hill that offered, in the near distance, a view of the shimmering blue sea. Jamie took in a breath. He'd never seen anything quite so beautiful.

"Anyway," he said, suddenly coming back to Rafael's story. "I thought this was supposed to be a story about superstition?"

"Jamie!" said Rafael. "I haven't even got to that bit yet!"

"Well, get on with it!" Jamie laughed. "We'll be at the beach in a minute and then I'll be too busy playing to talk!"

"It turns out that the dog was a stray and, because it had helped to score a goal, one of the Botafogo players adopted it and it became the mascot of the club, coming to every game. They called it Biriba.

"And you know what they did? If they were ever doing badly in a game and needed a break, they would let Biriba run on to the pitch and scamper all over the place until the referee stopped the game.

"The Botafogo players never helped to get Biriba under control, so it always took ages, and by the time the match got restarted, Botafogo had reorganized and were ready to make a comeback. It was such a good plan and the dog became so famous that other teams even threatened to kidnap Biriba. Or do you say dog-nap him?"

"I don't know!" laughed Jamie. "Fair enough, Rafa, that is a pretty good story."

Rafael grabbed Jamie's hand so hard that they both

stopped walking. Rafael was shaking his head and his face was going red with laughter.

"That's not the best bit!" he giggled. "One day before a really big match, all the players were in the dressing room, warming up, you know, talking tactics, making their plans for the game when, out of nowhere, Biriba, you know … did his … pee on the full-back's leg! Right there in the dressing room."

"No way!" said Jamie. "That's gross!"

"Anyway, so Botafogo end up winning the game … and the president of the club, the man in charge of the whole of Botafogo, gets to hear about what happened – that before the game Biriba had peed on the full-back's leg. Well, this president was so superstitious that, from that day on, he made it an actual order that BEFORE EVERY SINGLE GAME Biriba had to pee on the *same* defender's leg because it gave them good luck!"

The two boys had to stop. They were laughing too much.

"What? Every game the same player had to get peed on?!" said Jamie, in between his convulsions. "Imagine if that happened in the Premier League!"

"I know! I know!" said Rafael. "And to top it off, that year Botafogo won the league!! And everybody believed it was down to the peeing dog! You see – we know about being superstitious in Brazil!"

20

The Streets

The boys' laughter had only just subsided when they turned another corner and entered another set of streets.

Instinctively, Jamie understood that they had turned a corner in more than one way. He looked at Rafael, who was already staring at him.

"These are the poor streets," said Rafael. "This is what we call a favela."

Jamie looked around him. They had been walking less than five minutes from the luxurious area in which Rafael lived and yet, suddenly, they had reached a different world. Poverty seemed to drift through these streets like smoke in the air.

However, there, right in the middle of it all, looking as happy as anyone Jamie had ever seen in his life, were seven or eight kids, dashing around playing football.

Jamie was hypnotized by the scene. The kids – boys and girls of all different skin colours – were running barefoot along the gravelled street, chasing after a ball, which was clearly badly punctured. Their clothes were ripped, their faces and hair were very dirty ... and yet they seemed to be having such fun. The football they were playing seemed to be full of joy.

Suddenly, one of the kids kicked the ball in the direction of Jamie and Rafael and now all of the players were rampaging towards them. Without thinking, Jamie advanced towards the ball at the same time as the smallest and thinnest of the kids.

The little Brazilian boy, who was wearing a ripped and tattered old Brazil football top, got to the ball just before Jamie and knocked it right between Jamie's legs, gleefully shouting: *"Caneta! Caneta!!"*

Within seconds, all of the other kids were crowding around Jamie, laughing, pointing at his red hair and grabbing at his Hawkstone top.

And now, holding the punctured ball under his arm, the boy who had just done the *caneta* had returned too. He also started grabbing at Jamie's Hawkstone shirt. He seemed to want to take it from Jamie.

Jamie's body tensed. He would never allow anyone to take this top. Every part of him was ready to fight.

But Rafael put his arm around Jamie and walked him away from the group, waving back at the other kids as he did so.

"They are just interested in you because you are different," said Rafael. "You don't have to be scared of them."

"I wasn't scared!" replied Jamie, a little too eagerly.

"Good," said Rafael. "Because I wanted to show you these streets. Many people, they come to Rio and all they see – all they want to see – is the beach. But Rio is about the streets as much as it is about the beach. Only when you understand that do you start to understand our city. Oh, and by the way, *caneta* means n—"

"Nutmeg – I know," said Jamie, feeling a twinge of embarrassment at having had the ball knocked through his legs by a kid younger than him.

"Those kids can play," he acknowledged. "They had talent."

"Of course they have talent!" laughed Rafael. "They are Brazilian."

㉑

The Master

"What's wrong with here?" asked Jamie.

It seemed as good a spot as any. There was space on the beach and people playing football all around.

"No, we are not there yet," said Rafael, trekking ahead, further along the beach.

Jamie and Rafael had been walking along the beach for fifteen minutes but it felt like six hours. Jamie could feel his skin burning in the roasting sun and his throat was so dry he would have given his life savings to have just one glass of ice-cold water.

And all of this was to find this man. This mysterious person who was somehow going to help Jamie play football *Brazilian style*.

Jamie watched Rafael march on. He had no choice but to follow.

"Whoever this guy is, he better be worth it," Jamie muttered to himself.

"There!" said Rafael a few minutes later. "There he is! *Olá, Mestre!*"

He was shouting and waving to someone by the sea.

Jamie followed the line of Rafael's wave. He looked past the string of cafés with music blaring out, beyond the sunbathers strewn across the beach and on towards a group of kids near the sea.

Even from his vantage point, Jamie could see that all of the kids were practising their skills. They were displaying acrobatic ability, continuous concentration and sublime skill. And every single one of them was beaming with pleasure. This was something close to football heaven.

Standing next to the footballers, watching their every movement, stood a tall man with his arms folded. He had clearly heard Rafael's shouts but had not reacted in any way.

Then, after another minute, he said something to one of the players and began walking towards Rafael and Jamie.

Jamie could sense just by Rafael's reaction that this

was a significant person. He strained his eyes to get a closer look at the man as he approached.

There was something in the way that he moved along the sand of the beach so smoothly that reminded Jamie of a lion prowling its territory. His natural movements spoke of power, athleticism and strength. And yet, as he drew nearer still, Jamie recognized that this was not a young man. Perhaps he was about sixty. About the same age as Mike.

The man had a mane of long, thick greying black hair, which contrasted to the short, clipped beard that completed his lean, chiselled facial features. His skin was brown and creased from years in the sun but his green eyes seemed bright and inquisitive.

As the man drew within a few feet of the pair, Rafael looked at Jamie and smiled.

"Jamie," he said proudly. "Get ready to meet O Mestre – The Master."

22

"Your Feet Must Be Free"

"M-M-Mestre, th-th-is is J-J-Jamie," Rafael had said. "He wants to l-l-learn."

Mestre had smiled kindly at Rafael and gestured for the boys to follow him to the area by the sea where all the skills were being demonstrated.

Now, as he walked behind Mestre and Rafael, who seemed to know each other pretty well, Jamie could feel his feet starting to tingle. They wanted to do just one thing: kick a ball.

As soon as they arrived in the area where the other kids were practising their skills, Rafael sat down cross-legged in the sand, got his notepad out of his bag and began writing immediately.

Meanwhile, Jamie watched the boy next to him flick the ball into the air, trap it on the back of his neck, flick it back into the air and then bicycle kick it into the sea! Then he dived in and swam the front crawl with incredible strength to recover it. The boy seemed to be a mixture between Tarzan and a freestyle soccer-skills sensation!

Then Jamie looked at the girl next to him. She was balancing the ball on top of her head, walking down towards the sea and then back up the beach. She seemed so in control of her body. As she walked, her eyes were fixed firmly on the ball on her forehead and a smile was fixed firmly on her face.

These were just two of around forty kids all practising, demonstrating and perfecting different ball skills, a few of which Jamie had seen before on the internet but most of which were completely new to him.

Jamie shook his head at Rafael in delighted disbelief. This set-up – being part of a Brazilian skills school on the beach – was even more than he had been hoping for! Rafael simply looked up from his notepad, smiled and gave Jamie a big thumbs up in return.

Looking around him, Jamie quickly came to a conclusion: he could not spend much time amongst such skilful players without becoming at least a little more skilful himself.

And now Mestre turned his attention to Jamie. The man's green eyes reflected the deep, mysterious colour of the sea.

"Shall I go and get one of those balls?" Jamie asked, beaming from ear to ear.

Mestre shook his head. He was pointing to Jamie's trainers.

"Your feet," said Mestre, speaking English with an incredibly thick Brazilian accent. "This is where it all begins. They must be free. You must touch the ball with your feet. Listen to the word: FOOTball. It starts with the foot."

Jamie understood about fifty per cent of what Mestre was saying. He'd grasped enough, though, to work out that he should take off his trainers. However, within seconds of putting his feet down on the sand, the heat was scorching them.

"Oweeee!" he screamed, hopping from foot to foot. The other kids turned to look at Jamie and laughed. With his strange, jerky jumping movements, he rather looked as though he were doing some kind of funky dance.

"Use the sea to cool your feet," advised Mestre. "And then run to the café over there and ask them for my water."

The "café over there" was about half a mile away. By the time Jamie got back with Mestre's bottle of water, his face was the same colour as his hair – bright red – and his legs had been drained of all their energy; running in the sand felt different and more tiring than any other surface on which Jamie had run.

However, there was another even greater problem.

"The soles of my feet are completely burnt!" Jamie complained. "I just tried to kick a ball and it was agony! How long will it take to heal?"

His question seemed to evoke a half smile from Mestre.

"You will play in a few days," he said.

"A few days?!" Jamie shouted in high-pitched anguish.

He was so confused. Back home, Mike encouraged him to play as often as possible, while this man … this *master*, seemed to be stopping him from playing.

"That's crazy!" Jamie snapped. "I need to play *now*!"

But Jamie's words seemed to have no impact on Mestre. They were like tiny grains of sand hitting a huge rock.

"You will play when you are ready. *Only* when you are ready," Mestre replied before turning away to focus on all his other pupils.

23

The Photo

"You have to trust him, Jamie," said Bernard. "He knows what he is talking about."

They had just finished dinner and Jamie had told Bernard that the only thing his feet had managed to do at the beach today was get burned.

"You know, Jamie," continued Bernard, "none of us would actually be here were it not for Mestre. Rafael has heard this story many times but I will tell it to you now. You see, when me and my parents came to Rio from São Paulo, I was twelve and I didn't know anyone. Not one person. Then, one day, I was walking on the beach and I saw all these other kids doing amazing football skills. They looked like they were having so much fun, so

I asked their teacher – the man we know as Mestre – if I could join in. He said I could, and that's how I made all my friends here. And one special friend in particular…"

Bernard looked at Rafael for a second and then continued.

"One of the girls who was learning with Mestre was a brilliant footballer, way better than me. I just thought she was the most amazing person I'd ever met. I knew I would marry her the first moment I saw her."

Bernard stopped talking for a second. He seemed to drift off into the distance before focusing again on Jamie.

"Because of that – the fact that Stephania, Rafael's mum, and I met while practising our skills – Mestre always says that Rafael is a child of football. It's a nice phrase, don't you think?"

Jamie nodded. And it was a nice phrase, but he couldn't help noticing the small tear that was rolling down Rafael's cheek. Jamie knew it was because he was missing his mum.

Bernard no doubt thought the same thing because he stood up and gave Rafael a really big hug and spoke some soft words to him in Portuguese.

"I'll leave you two to it," said Bernard softly. "And just have a little patience, Jamie. Mestre will know when you're ready."

Normally Jamie liked to stay up as late as possible. It was probably because he absolutely hated it when his mum told him he had to go to bed.

But tonight, Jamie actually wanted to go to bed. He wanted to read about the Legends of Brazilian Football in Mike's booklet.

"I'm going to bed," Jamie said, allowing himself an inward chuckle as he imagined his mum fainting at hearing him say those words.

"Yeah, me too," said Rafael, finally closing his notepad. "We were late today. We should get to Mestre early tomorrow. We have a lot to learn."

Jamie nodded and limped up the stairs. As he got to his bedroom door, he turned and looked downstairs to see Rafael pick up a framed photo by the banister and gaze at it.

Jamie had looked at that same photo during the day. It was a picture of Bernard and Rafael's mum standing together outside the front door of the house. They were both so happy. Both smiling so broadly.

Jamie watched as Rafael delicately kissed the photo before placing it carefully back down on the table.

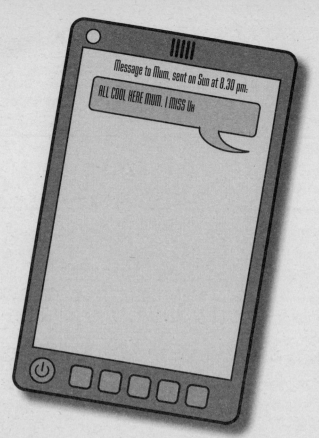

Message to Mum, sent on Sun at 8.30 pm:

ALL COOL HERE MUM. I MISS UX

Jamie's text had only been seven words long but he still squirmed a little when he sent it. Perhaps it was the kiss at the end. He didn't like the mushy stuff. His mum knew that he hated it when she kissed him in front of other people. But seeing Rafael kiss the photo of his mum had made Jamie think.

Yes, they had lots of arguments and yes, sometimes she really got on his nerves, but he couldn't for one second imagine what his life would be like without her.

THE LEGENDS OF
BRAZILIAN FOOTBALL

You would not believe how many wonderful players Brazil has had over the years, JJ. Zico, Sócrates, Ronaldo (the original one), Romário, Neymar...

The list is endless but, for me, by far the best are two attackers I used to watch when I was growing up. Their names were Pelé and Garrincha. Let me tell you, Jamie, these are two players whose names will live for ever. As people, they were as different from one another as you can imagine ... but as footballers, they had that quality that you and me always talk about and marvel at in the really best players - that extra little bit of magic.

Pelé was the son of a former professional footballer whose career was cut short by injury (remind you of anyone?) and so he devoted his life to having the career that his dad never did. He ended up winning the World Cup three times and scoring a thousand professional goals.

He became an idol all over the world, respected as quite possibly THE greatest of all time. There is a famous story that goes that one day in Brazil some very dangerous armed robbers tried to steal an expensive-looking car. But when they saw that Pelé was the driver, they politely apologized, hid their weapons and went on their way! Like I said: Pelé is a legend – for everyone!

But so is Garrincha – in a completely different way. While Pelé was the perfect athlete, respected like a god all over the world, Garrincha suffered from a physical deformity from birth ... which became his greatest strength. He was born with bent legs.

Although he looked like he would not even be able to run properly, the shape of Garrincha's legs actually meant that he could move in a unique way that no defender could guard against. He was impossible to tackle.

Once, he beat three defenders and the goalkeeper but, instead of kicking the ball into the empty net, he waited for the defenders to run back. As they sprinted towards him, Garrincha stepped out of their way, and one of them smacked straight into the goalpost! Then Garrincha decided to just walk the ball into the net!

Well, Jamie, that's it for now. We both know that you have a long road to walk before you can become a legend like these guys ... but boy are you in the right place to start!

PS I'm sure you'll learn your own
Portuguese while you're there. But here's a
word to kick you off. **Sim** - it means "yes".
So remember to shout that when you want
someone to pass you the ball!
Good luck, JJ ... and enjoy...

(24)

Rhythm of the Game

Monday 26 May

"Good!" said Mestre, looking at Jamie's feet. Overnight the rawness had started to heal and was beginning to be replaced by a thick outer layer of skin. "Soon your feet will be ready."

"Soon?" asked Jamie.

"Today we make your body ready," announced Mestre, before he shouted something to one of the café owners on the beach. "Can you dance?"

Jamie looked at Rafael for some assistance. What was going on now? But Rafael, who was noting everything down in his pad, half-smiled, half-chuckled back in Jamie's direction. He was offering no help.

Jamie shook his head vigorously. He hated dancing more than anything. He remembered his Aunt Suzy trying to make him dance at one of his mum's birthday parties. She had thrown him around the room, pulling him and pushing him all the time, with her hot and sweaty arms bumping into him. It felt like some kind of physical attack.

"Rosária!" called Mestre towards the girl who Jamie had seen balancing the ball on her head yesterday. His deep voice seemed to coast along the sea breeze because, even with the distance, the girl immediately stopped the skill she was practising, looked up and smiled.

Jamie had not noticed quite how pretty she was yesterday – he had been too overwhelmed by her skill to observe anything else. Yet now, as she skipped towards Mestre, juggling the ball perfectly in the air, Jamie was absolutely struck by her.

The girl, who looked about fourteen, smiled at Mestre, giving him a hug and a kiss. Jamie heard her use the word "Papa". Even he knew what that meant.

A few quick words of Portuguese followed between them and then a nod from the girl to Mestre, after which she began walking towards Jamie.

Jamie felt his whole body tighten. He was unable to swallow or move.

"*Olá!* I'm Rosária," she said, sparkling brighter than any star Jamie had ever seen, as she shook his hand.

"J-J-J ... Jamie," Jamie stammered. *Welcome to Rafael's world*, he thought.

And then the music began. All of a sudden, and from all of the cafés, there was loud samba music being blasted along the whole beach.

As if part of a game of musical chairs, as soon as they heard the sounds, practically everyone on the beach got up and began dancing! Out of nothing, there was now a full-scale party going on.

"Come," smiled Rosária, moving towards Jamie. "You dance with me."

"Errr!" Jamie winced, his voice going higher than it had been when he was five years old. "No – I'm OK, thanks!"

He tried to step away and find some place where he could hide, only to bump into the solid presence of Mestre, who was standing directly behind him.

"You want to learn how we play in Brazil?" he said. "Then you need rhythm."

With that, Rosária put her hands on Jamie's hips and started to guide his body to move in time with the beat. It felt seriously awkward. Especially with her dad watching.

He looked again at Rafael, who was now filming

what was happening on his phone. Jamie shrugged and forced a smile at the camera, to which Rafael responded by giving Jamie a big thumbs up.

Jamie was so nervous. This was nothing like dancing with his Aunty Suzy. This was a proper girl. He'd never danced with a real girl like this. He bet if he'd ever tried suggesting to Jack that they should dance together she would probably have kicked him in the shins!

But now, here he was, dancing to Brazilian music on the beach with one of the most beautiful girls he had ever seen. And she was three years older than him!

"Sorry!" said Jamie. He'd stepped on Rosária's toes for the fifth time in three minutes. Everyone else on the beach was doing professional twists and turns, while Jamie was moving like an Egyptian mummy, as though his body were frozen in time.

"Close your eyes," Rosária whispered softly in his ear. "Forget everything, OK? Hear only the music."

Jamie tried. He really did. But he just couldn't get it. When Rosária moved left, he moved right. When she took a step towards him, he did the same. Instead of gliding smoothly across the sand, their bodies were clashing and banging into each other like dodgem cars at a fairground.

"It's no good," he said after ten minutes of torture. "I haven't got rhythm. Let's just accept it. Some of us, like you, have got it. Some of us, like me, don't, and nothing you can do will change that. Now can we forget it and start working on some skills?"

He started to turn away.

"Everyone has the rhythm!" laughed Rosária, clasping Jamie's hot sweaty hand in her cool palm. "It's in there. We just have to find it."

25

Let Your Feet Feel the Beat

"Here," said Rosária. "Touch this. Put your hand on it."

Jamie knew that was what she said by reading her lips. He certainly couldn't hear the words themselves.

They were standing outside one of the beach cafés, directly next to a humongous speaker. Rosária had dragged him here and was now placing his hand on the enormous, vibrating sound system.

"Can you feel it now?" she shouted.

"Feel what?" roared Jamie, trying to make himself heard above the din.

"The beat! You have been listening to the melody. Forget the melody. Your feet need to feel the beat!"

With that, she placed her hand on top of Jamie's and

pressed them both down hard on the speaker.

The pulse of the music was making the speakers move, sending waves of strong vibrations through their hands.

"Can you feel it now?" she asked, pushing Jamie's hand down even harder on the speaker.

Jamie nodded.

"I can feel it!" Jamie shouted. "I can feel the beat insi—"

Rosária put her finger on Jamie's lips to stop him speaking.

Jamie carried on mumbling but Rosária wouldn't let any more words tumble from his mouth.

"Don't talk," she said. "Just relax. Just dance. Good... Goood!... *Ginga!*"

Jamie could have sworn the last word she said was "ginga". That was what people sometimes called him when they were being mean about his red hair.

He looked up at her accusingly but she was still smiling kindly back at him. She did not look as though she was teasing him now. In the midst of the loud music, he must have heard the word wrong.

He smiled back at her and made sure he concentrated on keeping the beat...

"OH. MY. GOD," Jamie said to Rafael, wiping the

sweat from his forehead as he gulped down a whole bottle of water. The music had just stopped. "How long have we been going?"

"About f-four hours," said Rafael.

"Four hours!" said Jamie, spitting out his drink.

"Well, how long did you think it had been?"

"I don't know – an hour, maybe."

"Time flies when you're having fun, eh?"

Jamie nodded. It had been fun all right. He could see now why Mike had always dreamed of dancing the samba all night. Brazilians were experts at knowing how to enjoy themselves. At one point, while they were dancing, a whole group of people had even gathered around to watch Jamie and Rosária, clapping all their moves.

"Look out," said Rafael. "She's c-coming over."

"*Obrigada*," said Rosária, giving Jamie the smallest of kisses on both of his cheeks.

Jamie smiled and nodded back to her. He didn't feel like a shy and nervous little boy any more.

"*Obrigada* yourself, Rosária," he said, trying to sound extra smooth as he ran his fingers through his hair. "So..."

"No, Jamie!" laughed Rosária. "Girls say *obrigada*, you say *obrigado* ... unless you are a girl. You are not a girl, are you, Jamie?"

"No! Oh my God no!" said Jamie, his temporary coolness shattered in an instant. "I promise I'm not a girl – I just—"

But it was too late. Rosária was already making her way back to the skills area, leaving Jamie to ask himself two questions: did that all actually just happen?

And what on earth did any of it have to do with football?

26

Just Like Ronaldo

"You know," grinned Rafael. "I reckon you've got a thing for girls who play football!"

They were walking home from the beach and Jamie was still bouncing along to the rhythm inside his head.

"Shut up, Rafa!" he said, giving his companion a friendly shoulder barge for good measure.

"It's true! There's Jack at home, and now you obviously think Rosária is the most beautiful girl you've ever seen!"

"I said: *shut up*!" laughed Jamie.

"Don't worry, I'm just jealous – I didn't get a kiss, did I? And anyway, you're not the only one. Ronaldo was the same."

"Ronaldo?" said Jamie. "Which one?"

"The original Ronaldo. The Brazilian one. He once met this girl called Milene. She was phenomenal at football, I mean like record-breaking phenomenal. She once did fifty-five thousand kick-ups."

"Shut up!" Jamie repeated. "That is no way true."

"Swear on my life," said Rafael. "Look it up when we get home. Her name is Milene Domingues and she set that world record for kick-ups when she was seventeen! And guess what else?"

"What?"

"She was a model."

"No way."

"Yes way. And guess what else? She played for the Brazil Women's National Team. And guess what else?"

"There's more?"

"Ronaldo married her!"

"I'm not surprised!" said Jamie.

"Yeah," laughed Rafael. "I mean, they got divorced in the end but when they were married they actually played football together. I bet you'd like that wouldn't you, Jamie – playing football with your wife!"

"I'd just like to play football with anyone at the moment," he said.

Although he'd had a brilliant day dancing on the beach, a part of Jamie remained disappointed. He still hadn't actually played football yet and it was killing him.

"I mean, I'm not being funny or anything," said Jamie, turning the subject away from football-playing supermodels. "But do we even know that Mestre is that good at football himself? I haven't seen *him* kick a ball yet."

Rafael gave Jamie a withering look.

"You are my friend, Jamie," said Rafael. "But sometimes you ask all the wrong questions."

They were now passing through the streets where the poorer kids were playing football again.

"Hey!" Jamie said to Rafael, his face suddenly brightening. "This is perfect. I can play with these guys!"

Jamie put down his bag and went to do up his laces nice and tight. The soles of his feet still hurt a bit … but not enough to stop him playing. This would be great – playing with the street kids on their own turf…

"No," said Rafael, putting his hand on Jamie's shoulder. "It's not safe for you to play here."

"What are you talking about, not safe?" said Jamie. "They're just kids like us – that's what you said yesterday. They won't do anything to me."

"It's not the players," explained Rafael. "That is not the reason. Look at their pitch."

Jamie looked at the ground that the kids were playing on. Initially, he saw nothing wrong, but then when he looked closer, his eyes started to pick up the detail. The ground was covered in bits of stone, rocks and even animal bones. And yet the kids were still playing barefoot.

"Right," said Jamie, his voice dropping. The last thing he needed was to sprain his ankle on a bit of rock and end up in hospital. His mum would have a nervous breakdown. "Well, can we at least watch for a bit?"

"Of course," smiled Rafael, taking out his notepad.

Jamie and Rafael had watched the street kids playing for about half an hour. Jamie saw how they deftly evaded the rocky debris and admired their touches of street skill as they nimbly nipped past one another.

Towards the end of the game, the smallest, thinnest boy wearing the same old, ripped Brazil shirt had once again spotted Jamie and approached him. Again, he had tugged at Jamie's shirt. Again, Jamie had refused, but he had smiled at the boy and looked into his eyes.

The boy's face was so dirty and his frame was painfully thin and yet his eyes were clear and expressive. It was an image that had remained fixed in Jamie's mind.

"Rafa, can I ask you a question?" said Jamie, still

thinking about the boy as they turned into the plush suburb where Bernard's house was.

"Go ahead," said Rafael.

"Well, if everyone in your country loves football, if the whole of Brazil is obsessed by the game ... and if there are lots of rich people in houses like this ... then why do those kids have to play ... like *that*?"

Rafael looked at Jamie. He seemed a little shocked.

"You are right, Jamie," said Rafael. "And you know, my mum always used to ask the same question."

27

All in the Notepad

Jamie looked into Rafael's room. His friend was sitting at his desk, lost in another world as he scribbled furiously in his notepad. In all the time that they had known each other, Jamie had still never seen him without it.

Jamie was desperate to know what Rafael wrote in that notepad. He knew it was to do with football because when, yesterday, Jamie had asked Rafael if he ever played football, Rafael said that he used to when he was younger – and that he was an OK player – but that now he preferred to study the game. Jamie had noticed that when Rafael said the word "study" he had subconsciously tapped his notepad.

It was all in there. Jamie just didn't know what *it* was. Part of him was tempted to steal the pad for a minute when Rafael wasn't looking just to sneak a peek at what was inside, but Jamie knew he would never do that. He would only ever see what was inside the notepad if Rafael let him.

Jamie went downstairs, noticing immediately how springy his feet felt against the carpet. The burns were nearly healed and it was almost as if the outer layer of skin had evolved into a new tougher, harder membrane that now covered the inner, more sensitive part of his foot.

"How's it going?" asked Bernard, who was sitting in the kitchen, as Jamie helped himself to a glass of milk from the fridge. The milk somehow tasted different to home – a little sweeter, perhaps.

"So, so," said Jamie. "It's been good and everything … but I haven't actually kicked a ball yet…"

It was only when he'd finished speaking that Jamie realized that Bernard might not have been talking about football. He might have been referring to Rafael's stammer, wondering whether his son was any closer to speaking freely in public.

That was a difficult question to answer. On the face of it, there had been no progress: Rafael still hadn't spoken to anyone in public – or even his dad – without a stammer. Yet when it was just him and Jamie, it was now impossible to shut him up! The boy had turned into a complete chatterbox!

"Oh, by the way," said Bernard, changing the conversation. "You should go and get your jacket on. We're leaving in ten minutes."

"Huh?" said Jamie. "Where we going?"

"To watch some football," replied Bernard. "Some real Brazilian football."

Really at the Game

Palmeiras v Santos
At the Estádio do Pacaembu
São Paulo

The sound hit Jamie like a wall.

He was right in the middle of a sea of forty thousand football-mad Brazilians, all of whom were singing, smiling and banging their drums, all ready for the beginning of the game.

As they took their seats, Jamie watched Bernard giving Rafael a big hug. It reminded him of when he and Mike went to watch Hawkstone. There was something special about going to football matches, something that brought people closer together. This must be the big event that they had to come home for, Jamie thought to himself. And he could understand why. To be here, at a top Brazilian football match, was well worth travelling across the globe for.

Jamie looked around him. Men, women, boys and girls ... all ages, all colours, all races – all singing and happy ... all dressed in Palmeiras's famous white and green strip. They had completely forgotten their normal lives. They were just here to enjoy the game. *This is a carnival of football*, Jamie thought. *And I'm part of it!*

Jamie was shouting for Palmeiras just as loud as if he had been at a Hawkstone match back home. And almost from the very kick-off, there was a lot for Jamie to cheer; the match rained goals!

It seemed as though each time one of the sides scored, the other would just go up the other end and equalize. It was everything Jamie could have hoped for: goals, skills and celebrations. He was up from his seat every five minutes, clapping, roaring his approval and giving Rafael a massive high five and hug each time Palmeiras scored.

By half-time, the game was already 3-3, one of the highest-scoring forty-five minutes Jamie had ever seen. Rafael was using the break to update his notepad while Bernard went to get them some drinks.

*

Everything was just about perfect. However, Jamie was not smiling. In fact, there was something that had really started to annoy him and it was beginning to make him angry too: practically all the fans around him had been taking the mickey out of him for the whole of the first half.

Right from the moment they had arrived, just as the game kicked off, and all the way through the match itself, many of the people sitting around Jamie had been shouting "ginga" at him.

Jamie hadn't liked it when he thought that Rosária had used the word at the beach and he liked it even less now.

He knew that there weren't many people with bright red hair like him in Brazil and he accepted the fact that it made him look different to everyone else. But to single him out and shout "ginga!" at him really loudly AND laugh and clap while they did it … well, that was completely out of order. He could feel his anger rising again. He knew he had to say something; otherwise he might lose his temper.

"Can you please tell them to stop?" Jamie asked Bernard as soon as he came back with the drinks.

"I hate it. It's mean and I can't enjoy the game properly with them shouting 'ginga' at me the whole time because of my hair."

Bernard and Rafael both looked at each other and raised their eyebrows.

"Do you want to tell him or shall I?" Bernard asked Rafael.

Rafael pointed to his dad. He had started laughing.

"OK. It's not exactly what you think, Jamie," said Bernard. Even he was nearly smiling too. "In Brazil, *ginga* is nothing to do with hair. It is a word which means something else here. It describes the skills, the joy, the personality needed in order to make beautiful football.

"We say *ginga* when Ronaldo cheekily dribbles past three defenders and the goalkeeper before back-heeling the ball into the net. *Ginga* is when Ronaldinho smiles before flicking the ball over your head and volleying it in ... and *ginga* can also be the way you sway your hips when you are dancing...

"It is a rhythm, a feeling – a kind of joy – so when the fans are saying it, they are not talking about you, they are cheering for the players, to give them a mood to bring out the *ginga* in the air, to let it sweep from the terraces to the pitch."

"Oh, right," said Jamie, suddenly feeling a little foolish. "Well, if it's not about me ... I guess that's OK, then."

*

Once Jamie knew what ginga meant, he enjoyed the second half way better ... and so did the Palmeiras fans, because, having gone 4-3 down, they managed to come back to win 5-4 in spectacular fashion.

When Arnaldo's winning bicycle-kick goal went in, Jamie actually thought one of his eardrums might burst, such was the noise generated by everyone within the stadium.

"Gol! Gol! Gol! Gol! Gol! Gol! Gol! Gol! Gol! Gol! Gol! Gol! Gol! Gol! Gol! Arnaldo!!!! Gol! Gol! Gol! Gol! Gol! Gol! Gol! Gol! Gol! Gol! Gol!" shouted the commentator, who was sitting a few seats back from Bernard and the boys. The man was going completely mental.

Jamie and Rafael turned to look; he was standing up, his face was bright red and he screaming into his microphone, still repeating: *"Gol! Gol! Gol! Gol! Gol! Gol! Gol! Gol! Gol! Goooooooooooooool!"*

He must have done it about a hundred times. Jamie and Rafael laughed and immediately tried to copy him. They got up to forty before having to stop through complete exhaustion.

As they made their way back to the car from the stadium amidst all the other fans, Jamie felt as if he was floating across the ground. Back home, when he tried to explain to people (other than Mike and Jack) how he felt about football; how much he loved the game, how it was in his mind the whole time, they didn't understand. They just told him things would change when he discovered girls. They had no idea.

It was only now, only after he had been to see a real, live game here, that Jamie understood why Brazil was just about the best country in the world. Not only did everyone here understand his love for football, they all felt the same way!

㉙ Opening Up

"Thank you so much! That was the best game that I have ever seen in my life!" beamed Jamie when they got home.

It had also been one of the longest car journeys of his life – nearly five hours all the way back to Rio from São Paulo – and it was now nearly three o'clock in the morning, but Jamie was still wide awake … and he wasn't the only one.

Sitting around the kitchen table, eating pastries filled with hot, creamy chicken (a dish called *pastel frito de frango*, Jamie had learned), the three of them were still talking about the incredible game they had witnessed. Or rather, Jamie was talking and the other two were listening because, while Bernard nodded and Rafael scribbled away in his notepad, Jamie unleashed a relentless review of every thought that was popping into his head.

"Now I can say I've seen a top match in Brazil! Mike is going to go ballistic when I tell him!" he said proudly, almost shouting, even though the other two people in the room were sitting at the same table as him.

"And I can always say that I saw Arnaldo play when he was really young. You were right, Rafa – he was amazing! He'll definitely get signed by a European club in the next transfer window. Talk about tekkers! That bicycle kick was insane. I mean, how do you actually become *that* good? He was literally ON ANOTHER LEVEL!

"I'll tell you what *I* want to know, though," continued Jamie. "What did the Palmeiras manager do to change it when they went 4-3 down? It was like he switched the entire team formation and then they went and won 5-4. How did he do it?"

Jamie finally allowed himself a breath and a big gulp of water. Then he suddenly noticed Bernard looking at Rafael.

"Go on," said Bernard to his son. "Why don't you show him, Rafa?"

Rafael stopped writing in his notepad and looked up.

There was a second of silence as he looked at his dad, then at Jamie and then back down at his notepad. He seemed to be weighing up the most important decision of his life.

And then, extremely slowly and extremely carefully, Rafael got up, came to sit next to Jamie, and held open his notepad for Jamie to see the pages.

Jamie stared at what was in front of him. His eyes widened and his mouth hung open.

He was looking at the most advanced, analytical and complex football sketches that he had ever seen.

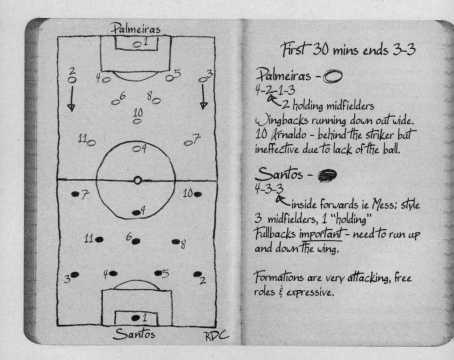

First 30 mins ends 3-3

Palmeiras - ◯
4-2-1-3
↖ 2 holding midfielders
Wingbacks running down out wide.
10 Arnaldo - behind the striker but ineffective due to lack of the ball.

Santos - ●
4-3-3
↖ inside forwards ie Mess; style
3 midfielders, 1 "holding"
Fullbacks important - need to run up and down the wing.

Formations are very attacking, free roles & expressive.

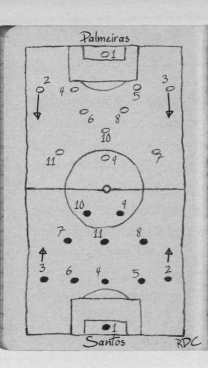

Palmeiras

Santos

RDC

Second 30 mins
ends 4-3 to Santos

Palmeiras - ○
4-2-1-3 (same)

Santos - ●
5-3-2 (change)
3 defenders with 2 wingbacks.
Dominate midfield due to the extra
(3rd) man.

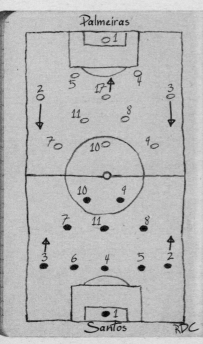

Palmeiras

Santos

RDC

Last 30 mins 5 - 4 - Full time
How Palmeiras won it.

Palmeiras 2-3-2-3
Santos 5-3-2

Only 2 defenders (a gamble) but have
more numbers in the midfield to dominate possession. If Palmeiras have it
Santos can't score.

Key Change - 10 Arnaldo moved to
central attacking position, so all play
and chances come to him.

<u>Magic Moment</u> — Arnaldo's winning goal.
Intricate midfield passing. Jadson (3)
advances and crosses deep. Ball at
wrong height for Arnaldo, who changes
his body position, leaps into the air,
scissor kicks in top left corner! Gol!
Gol! Gol!

Across the pages were three images in total, representing the three thirty-minute phases that totalled the full ninety-minute match they had just watched. Each diagram depicted how the two teams were structurally set up for that period, detailing their formation, tactics and passing movements.

Together, the three drawings faultlessly reproduced the entire story of the game from a tactical point of view and explained just how Palmeiras had pulled off a tactical masterstroke, enabling them to come back and win the game.

It was just about the most beautiful piece of work that Jamie had ever seen in his life. It was science, art and football all combined.

"Oh my God!" said Jamie, snatching the notepad out of Rafael's hands. "Let me see that!"

Jamie took hold of the notepad and flicked through the pages. Everything he saw was the same level. It was the work of a genius. Quickly, Jamie turned another page and saw himself. Or rather, a diagram of himself, with key analysis of all his strengths and weaknesses as a player.

"Rafa! Can I keep this for the night? It's ama—"

But then Jamie stopped talking. Because he had seen Rafael's face.

"G-G-G-Give it b-b-b-b-b-back!" Rafael shouted,

grabbing the notepad from Jamie, tearing one of the pages in the process.

Jamie looked at himself in the full-length mirror on the inside of the cupboard door. He was in his bedroom. There was just a thin wall separating him from Rafael. He had knocked on Rafael's door but it had been locked and Rafael hadn't responded to Jamie's pleas to let him come in. So Jamie had gone to his own bedroom instead.

It was such a nice, spacious room with a high ceiling, big cupboards and a beautiful wide bed. If he had a bedroom this size at home he would feel so lucky and happy. So different to how he felt now.

Jamie looked at his face in the reflection. The pale freckled skin. The darting blue eyes. Why did he hate himself sometimes? Why? Because he ruined everything.

Rafael was the kindest, most gentle boy he had ever met. He had trusted Jamie enough to open up to him like no one else and he had invited Jamie into his world; made it possible for Jamie to come to Brazil, made a dream come true.

And how had Jamie repaid him? By trying to take too much. By snatching the notepad away when Rafael had only wanted him to look at it and breaking every element of trust that they had established between them.

Jamie could hear Rafael crying next door. He knew he had ruined it all now. Just like he ruined everything. Anything good that ever happened in his life, he had to ruin it. No wonder his dad had left. He had been right to; right to get away from Jamie … right to get as far away as possible.

Jamie looked again. Looked again at his own face and watched as, in his mind's eye, it began to turn into his dad's face. Then he felt the anger coming again … building like a tidal wave. He forced himself to look again – just one more time. It was disgusting. He hated his own face. He wanted it gone.

The glass shattered upon the impact of Jamie's first, venomous kick. The shards flew everywhere and, before he knew it, Jamie was sitting on the bed, watching Bernard rush in to pick up the pieces.

"I bet you're wishing you'd never invited me here. I'm so sorry. I can't believe I broke the mirror," said Jamie, helping Bernard to pick up the splinters of broken glass. His anger had gone now. Just sadness about what he had done remained.

"Look," Bernard said. "Forget about the mirror. There are just some things … that you don't know.

That notepad is very precious to Rafael. Just before she died, Stephania gave it to him because she knew how much he liked writing and drawing his football notes … so that's why he reacted like he did when you took it. I think he felt like you were taking a bit of her away … and I'm not sure he's ready to let her go yet."

Jamie shook his head. He knew about letting parents go – or, in his case, a dad letting *him* go – but that was still no excuse to have smashed the mirror.

"In fact, I think you should be proud," continued Bernard. "It's a very big deal for Rafa to open up his notepad and show it to someone. Aren't the drawings incredible?"

"Incredible," Jamie repeated. "And I ruined it."

"No," responded Bernard, shaking his head. "You're being too hard on yourself. You'll only ruin it if you stop or change now. Just get him talking again. That's how you can make up for it. When he is hurt, this is when he stops talking … but we can't let him go into his shell again. Now more than ever is the time for you to encourage Rafael to talk again."

30
Brothers

Tuesday 27 May

"Your dad told me about the notepad..." said Jamie, hesitatingly. "That your mum gave it to you."

He and Rafael were walking to the beach as normal, but neither of them had said a word to each other yet today.

They had both eaten their cereal in silence, Jamie stealing covert looks at his friend in the process. Rafael had dark bags under his eyes and Jamie suspected that he might not have slept all night.

He'd been trying to work out what to say to Rafael, how to earn his trust again, but it was difficult. Jamie had never been great with words so he hadn't said any. Until now.

"I should never have tried to touch it," said Jamie.

Rafael nodded but he didn't look at Jamie. Bernard was right. He had gone back into his shell. They carried on walking in silence.

Just one word. That was all Jamie needed. Rafael had been talking so much since they had got to Brazil ... if he would just start talking again, Jamie was sure that they could pick up where they'd left off.

He reached deep into himself to look for something that might bring Rafa back. Then he remembered something that Mike always said: *the more you give, the more you get*.

"Can I tell you something I've never told anyone before?" asked Jamie, feeling a bundle of nerves begin to sprout within him.

Rafael nodded.

"Every day ... when I wake up, the first thing that I do, before anything else, is pray that, one day, my dad will come back," said Jamie.

He talked quietly, and when he'd finished speaking, his mouth curved downwards. It was true – he *did* do that every day ... and he *had* never told anyone.

Rafael stopped walking and turned to look at Jamie. It was the kind of look that only brothers normally give each other.

Silence stood between them.

"B-b-b-but you know he never w-will," whispered Rafael, finally speaking for the first time that day.

Jamie shook his head. A tear wet his eye.

"It's been nearly t-t-two years now," said Rafael. "And you know, my d-dad hasn't smiled once – not properly – since sh-sh-she…"

Jamie thought back to Bernard's broad smile in that photo of him and Stephania at the house. It was such a big smile, that it looked as though it should last for ever.

"Life sucks sometimes, doesn't it?" said Jamie. "But it gets better. It never stops hurting … but it does get better."

(31)
Ready

Jamie and Mestre looked at each other, each bearing a steely glare; each unwilling to give way.

Jamie had once again asked to start working with the ball. Mestre had once again told him he was not ready.

Then Jamie felt the cord snap inside him. *Ready ...* why did he keep going on about being "ready"?

"Fine!" said Jamie, picking up his stuff. "It doesn't even matter whether you think I'm ready because I don't need you! I'm in Brazil – the home of football – I can play football on the beach with anyone I want!"

With that, Jamie began stomping up the beach. His outburst had not soothed his anger, only inflamed it.

"You should come back," said Rafael, sprinting to try and keep up with Jamie. "You're making a mistake."

"The only mistake was wasting two whole days listening to his stupid ideas," snapped Jamie. "Like I'm going to go home and tell Jack and Mike: *yeah, I was in Brazil but no, I didn't actually play football.*"

It was only the huge commotion that was occurring further up the beach that pulled Jamie out of his anger for a second. About fifty yards away, lots of people were making noise and shouting and clapping. They seemed to be aiming their attention in one direction, towards one particular person.

Jamie focused his eyes and made out a figure walking towards him down the beach. The person was being followed and cheered as he walked.

Indeed, it was the walk – the athletic grace of it – that gave away the person's identity. Jamie had recognized him seconds before he could hear the cheers that were accompanying him.

"Arnaldo! Arnaldo!" the people were singing, as the best young footballer in the whole of Brazil walked down the beach.

Then something absolutely incredible happened: Arnaldo began to smile and wave … in Jamie's direction!

Jamie could not believe it. This was way beyond his wildest dreams.

He smiled and waved back as the heroic figure drew nearer still … and then watched as Arnaldo walked past him.

It hadn't been Jamie that he had been waving at.

Jamie turned around to see where he was heading … it was straight towards Mestre. What did Arnaldo want with the old man?

"Mestre!!" Arnaldo was now shouting, quickening his pace to give the Master a high five. *Meu amigo!*

Mestre and Arnaldo give each other a huge hug and immediately began laughing together. It was like a child greeting his favourite uncle.

Jamie shook his head in utter disbelief.

"Can we talk to him, Rafa?" he asked. "Can we talk to Arnaldo?"

"Well, that depends," said Rafael. "Last thing I remember is you shouting your mouth off at the man who taught him everything he knows!"

(32) Meeting the Man

"There's so much I want to ask you!" said Jamie, feeling his body tingle with excitement. "That magic in your play, please tell me how you get it!"

Mestre and Arnaldo were sitting on a couple of deckchairs watching the kids by the sea perfecting their skills. When Jamie had apologized for losing his temper, Mestre had just laughed and said: "It's good. This is what a footballer needs – passion!"

Mestre explained that ten years ago Arnaldo had been just like Jamie and the other kids: one of Mestre's pupils on the beach.

Arnaldo himself had nodded.

"Eh…" Arnaldo said, looking at Jamie. "You learn with Mestre now, yes?"

Jamie nodded enthusiastically but, inside, he was full of embarrassment. He couldn't believe that a few minutes ago he had been prepared to turn his back on Mestre. This was the man who had taught Arnaldo – and Jamie had got in a huff with him! What a waste it would have been if he had stormed off … what a mistake. Maybe Jack and his mum were right; perhaps he did need to work on keeping his temper under control.

"And you have been running on the beach?"

"Sure have," Jamie grinned.

"And you have been dancing?"

"Yup," confirmed Jamie.

Arnaldo began laughing. He stood up and started doing some samba moves in front of Mestre. He even tried to pull Mestre up from his seat to dance too but Mestre was having none of it.

"Mestre!" said Arnaldo, now laughing even harder. "So now it is time for him to play footvolley?"

Mestre got to his feet and smiled.

"OK," he said finally. "The British boy has passion. So now we see if he is ready."

Mestre and Rosária were on one side of the net, warming up, with Arnaldo waiting for Jamie to join him on the other side. Jamie was on his way; he was just getting some instructions from Rafael, who had asked if he could have a minute to tell Jamie all the rules.

"Footvolley is basically a mixture between volleyball and football," he explained. "There is a court marked out in the sand, which you can see, there is a net and there are two players on each side; in this case, you and Arnaldo versus Mestre and Rosária."

Jamie grinned. He loved it when Rafael said the words "you and Arnaldo".

"Listen, Jamie, this is important!" said Rafael. "There are lots of people watching, you are going to want to play well. You can use any part of your body to control the ball and get it over the net apart from your hands. So, that basically means your feet, chest and head."

"Got it," Jamie said.

Looking at the intensity in Rafael's eyes, he suddenly felt as though he were being given a pre-match team-talk by a top coach. He realized again how much he liked and respected Rafael. He was so happy that they were talking again after what had happened last night.

"And remember," said Rafael. "Because you can't use your hands, it's very difficult to do a smash, so some of these rallies will go on for a very long time."

Jamie nodded again, shook Rafael's hand, took his place on the court and did a high five with Arnaldo. If he was completely honest, Jamie wasn't that worried or nervous because alongside him, as his partner, he had one of the best young footballers in the world. All Jamie had to do, he reasoned, was set the ball up for Arnaldo and this would be a pretty simple victory.

Not for the first time in his life, Jamie could not have been more wrong.

(33)

Golden Touch

The ball dropped perfectly, just over the net, and settled smoothly into the sand. It had been struck with such sweet softness that it had seemed to drop lightly towards the sand like a falling leaf.

Jamie and Arnaldo both collapsed, panting like wild dogs. Mestre had taunted and teased them by keeping every rally going for such a long time that, by the end, they were begging for it to be over.

Jamie had run and scampered as far and fast as he could. Arnaldo had shown some unbelievable touches but none of them had compared to the control of the ball that Mestre had demonstrated.

Every single touch of the ball he'd had had been pure

gold, including this last one, when he had deftly flicked it just over the net with the outside of his foot to win the game for him and Rosária.

Jamie felt a hand grab him and pull him up from the ground.

It was Arnaldo. He still wore the same smile that he'd had before the game.

"Don't worry that we lose," he grinned as he and Jamie shook hands with their opponents. "This is why we call him O Mestre!"

Jamie nodded. For the first time since he had arrived on the beach, he genuinely understood the truth of the situation.

On the other side of that net was a living, breathing master of football.

"He wouldn't tell me who he really was," revealed Jamie. "His real story…"

He and Rafael were just turning into the road of Rafael's house. Even though he had lost at footvolley, Jamie was feeling much better. After all, he had now kicked a ball! Yet this one question was still bugging him.

"After the game and once we all had our photo taken with Arnaldo, I went up to Mestre by myself and said to him: 'Your touch is better than any player I have ever seen, even the ones at Barca and Madrid. Why hasn't the whole world heard of you?'"

"And let me guess," laughed Rafael. "Mestre didn't tell you his story?"

"No," said Jamie. "He just looked at me and said that tomorrow he would start to show me the secrets. You must know his story, Rafa, if your dad has known him for so long. Come on, tell me … I've got to know!"

"He is exactly who he says he is," smiled Rafael, as though he knew more than he was prepared to tell Jamie. "He's the man who will show you the secrets of the Brazilian skills."

Night Mail

From:	**Jacqueline Marshall**
To:	**Jamie Johnson**
Date:	**28 May** **02.24**
Subject:	**Hey**

How's it going out there? Tell me stuff! By the way, I bumped into Ms Vetterlein in town today and she told me doesn't think she can play in the T v P game! Says Hawkstone's Women's Team have got a Cup Final that weekend and she can't risk it! Result! Say hi to Rafael for me.

J

From: Jamie Johnson
To: Jacqueline Marshall
Date: 28 May   02.28
Subject: The MOST amazing thing in the world EVER

OMG, Jack, can't believe you emailed me now – I was literally JUST about to email you… You will not believe this! Today at the beach, WE MET ARNALDO!!!

He's the best young player in Brazil and he is so cool. He's got this whole Mohawk thing going on with his hair… Anyway!!! We played this football volleyball game and I was on THE SAME SIDE as Arnaldo! Just me and him. We lost (I didn't realize at the time, but there's a guy on the beach who's some kind of legend or something and he's going to teach me Brazilian skills tomorrow) but anyway, it didn't matter, me and him were so cool together, just high fiving the whole time!

Got a photo too, just in case no one believes me! Sending it with this email – let me know what you think. Can't wait to see you and start planning our tactics for Teachers v Pupils. Love that Ms Vetterlein's not playing! Maybe I should ask my mate Arnaldo to come and play for us?!
JJ

From: Jacqueline Marshall
To: Jamie Johnson
Date: 28 May   02.32
Subject: Re: The MOST amazing thing in the world EVER

Awesome!! Definitely get him to play for us! Imagine Pratley's face when we turn up with Arnaldo on our side! ROFL just thinking about it!!
Who's the girl?

From: Jamie Johnson
To: Jacqueline Marshall
Date: 28 May   02.33
Subject: Re: The MOST amazing thing in the world EVER

That's Rosária, the legend's daughter. Amazing at football and she's taught me how to dance too! Got some serious moves now!

From: Jacqueline Marshall
To: Jamie Johnson
Date: 28 May   02.34
Subject: Re: The MOST amazing thing in the world EVER

How nice for you both

From: Jamie Johnson
To: Jacqueline Marshall
Date: 28 May   02.35
Subject: Re: The MOST amazing thing in the world EVER

Don't be like that, Jack! She's a really nice girl. Please don't get mad at me.

From: Jacqueline Marshall
To: Jamie Johnson
Date: 28 May   02.52
Subject: Re: The MOST amazing thing in the world EVER

Ha! Only pulling your leg! She seems really nice. Anyway, you can do what you want. You're not my boyfriend.
Yet.

(35)

Up in the Air

Wednesday 28 May

"There are many different types of football," said Mestre, his powerful, firm hand resting on Jamie's shoulder. "The beach is different to the rest because here it is difficult to dribble in the sand. Here, everything is about keeping the ball in the air. But you take these lessons from the beach and they work in any football ... you understand?"

"Yes, Mestre."

"Good – so now you try."

Without warning, Mestre volleyed a football hard at Jamie, who instinctively chested it up into the air and began juggling with both feet. He had just passed his first test of Brazilian beach football.

Soon, Rosária came to join him, and then three more players. They formed a small circle on the wet part of the sand just next to the sea. They were playing the most simple of football games – keeping the ball up. Each player was allowed just one touch with any part of their body (apart from their hands) and, collectively, their aim was to keep the ball in the air for as long as possible.

By watching the other players, Jamie quickly observed how they used their shoulders, heels, thighs and knees just as much as their feet. Each part of the body had its own shape and way of connecting with the ball. For example, the knee and heel were hard, giving good power and distance, while the thigh and chest were soft, offering more control.

New to Jamie too was the fact that they seemed to use the outside of their foot when touching the ball as much as the instep; not only did it allow the players to get so much more spin on the ball but it looked more fun too!

Above everything, though, the key was to never give up. Every ball was retrievable.

"You can make that one!" Rosária said to Jamie on one occasion that he had let the ball bounce into the sand.

"But it was too far away," appealed Jamie, sorry to have let the other players down. They had kept it up for a hundred and four touches. "I'd have to have dived face-first into the sand to keep that one up!"

"Yes!" said Rosária. "And what is the problem with that?!"

It was true. Jamie watched how the other players chased every ball down, diving into the air, running into the sea, leaping into the sand to kick, head or chest the ball back to a waiting member of the team.

The best part of it was that no one ever got injured because the sand or the water was always there to break their fall.

Jamie realized this when he made his first run into the sea, chasing down a ball at full pelt, skipping into the water and then launching himself into the air, producing a bicycle kick to arrow the ball back behind him to where the rest of the players were standing.

After he made contact with the ball, his whole body plunged into the refreshing blue Brazilian sea. It was like a cool, cleansing shower. Jamie blew the bubbles out of his nose and then, feeling his feet touch the sand, pushed himself back up and out of the water in one powerful movement.

He rose, refreshed, from the sea and then sprinted back on to the beach to carry on with the game.

As he did so, he saw Mestre nodding and smiling.

Now Jamie got it. Now he understood.

Or at least he was starting to.

(36)

One Last Trick

Saturday 31 May – three days later

"I can't believe it," Jamie said to Mestre. "Ever since I've been playing with you guys, the time has gone in a flash. I can't believe I have to go home tomorrow."

For the last three days, every second on the beach had been filled with football. All manner of games had been played: footvolley, keeping the ball up in the air, beachfootball … in each one the principle was the same – controlling the ball with every part of the body and keeping it in the air for as long as possible.

Initially, Jamie had found it difficult. At home, all the

coaches had always told him the same thing: "Keep the ball on the ground!"

That was how the Europeans did it; the Spanish, the Italians ... they generally passed the ball on the ground. This was different. This was about keeping it up, keeping it alive, by any means and any skill possible.

However, with each second, with each hour and with each day, Jamie had got better and better. By now, Jamie's last day, he had developed the skill to use every part of his body in his play. There was not a ball that he didn't believe he could keep in the air somehow.

It had reached the stage that the Brazilian beachgoers were now well used to seeing the small, pale British boy sprinting like a madman into the sea or diving head-first into the sand, to flick, kick or head the ball, just to keep a game going. Yes, it meant he got a face full of sand about ten times a day, but he could not have cared less.

Mestre was standing on the beach, looking at the sea, with Jamie juggling a ball alongside him.

"We are always here," said Mestre. "You can come and see us again."

Jamie nodded, but something inside told him that this was a once-in-a-lifetime trip.

"If I don't," said Jamie, catching the ball for a

second, "can you teach me one last trick? A special one? You see, when I get home, I'm going to play in a massive match at school and I'll be up against an extremely difficult opponent. I'll need a bit of magic to beat him."

Mestre turned and looked at Jamie. Although they had been getting closer and Mestre seemed to be happy with Jamie's progress, Jamie could still never tell what he was thinking ... and he had never seen this look in Mestre's eyes either.

"A Mágica," Mestre said after a while. "Rafael told you about A Mágica?"

They both turned and looked at Rafael who, as always, was making notes in his pad. He had worked just as hard as Jamie over the last few days – in a different way.

"No," said Jamie. "He hasn't told me anything. It was just a question I thought of now, I promise."

"OK, then! It is your last day – I will do it," said Mestre, standing up and walking over to a game of beach football that was happening further down by the sea. As he walked over, the other players all stopped and smiled and began debating which side would take Mestre.

Perhaps sensing what was about to happen, Rafael came and sat down next to Jamie and, for once, closed his notepad and set his eyes on the match in front of them.

"Do you know what he's going to do?" asked Jamie.

"Maybe," smiled Rafael. "But I've only heard about it. I've never actually seen it."

37

A Mágica

The first five minutes of the game were not dissimilar to the other games of beach football that Jamie had watched over the last couple of days: small dribbles through the sand, chips to teammates, acrobatic headers and volleys. And lots of smiles.

Then, with almost no warning, Mestre did something that seemed to turn the whole of football on its head. Literally.

In the middle of the game, with the ball at his feet, Mestre flicked it up from the ground on to his head. He then proceeded to run past every single member of the opposition team whilst bouncing the ball on top of his forehead.

When he got to the goal, he let the ball drop from his head and volleyed it home.

All of the players in the game and Jamie and Rafael, watching from the sidelines, stood and clapped. It was both the most daring and effective bit of skill that Jamie had ever seen.

"What *was* that?" shouted Jamie. "He just dribbled the whole pitch with the ball on his head!"

"Yup," smiled Rafael, excitedly opening his notepad to start drawing. "And because the ball was on his head, no one could tackle him."

While Rafael was working, Jamie stood up and did the only thing in the world he could possibly think of doing now. He tried to replicate the skill he had just witnessed.

"Don't worry," said Mestre, walking past Jamie back to his seat. The beach football game had just finished and Jamie had failed to do the skill – for the twentieth time. In each attempt, he had managed to get the ball on his head, but it fell off as soon as he tried to walk with it, let alone run.

"You will not be able to do it," stated Mestre. He was speaking as a matter of fact rather than as a boast. "All my pupils have tried to do it – even Arnaldo – but no one is able. That is why I call it A Mágica."

"But I *want* to do it!" said Jamie. "It's amazing; impossible to defend against. Please teach me!"

Mestre shook his head. "It's impossible," he said. "It takes so much more time and we have none."

Jamie felt a hand on his shoulder and looked around. He was surprised to see that Bernard had come to pick him and Rafael up. They were flying home later that evening – perhaps he wanted to save on time.

Mestre smiled and nodded to Bernard. They said a few words to each other that Jamie could not understand and then Mestre gave Bernard a hug.

Now Mestre held out his strong hand for Jamie to shake.

"Good luck," he said. "You have learned the skills of the beach well. One day, if you come back, perhaps I can teach you A Mágica. Otherwise, it is impossible."

Jamie smiled and shook Mestre's hand firmly. It was strange; when he had first arrived at the beach, Jamie had thought that Mestre was the complete opposite of Mike, and yet now, somehow, he reminded Jamie of his granddad … perhaps just the Brazilian version.

"Thank you, Mestre," Jamie said. "I will remember and practise everything you've taught me."

And it was true. Although he had only had a few days learning from Mestre, the skills that he learnt on that beach – how to use every part of his body, how to play with rhythm and imagination – would stay with Jamie for ever.

But you're wrong about one thing, Jamie thought as the football computer in his head replayed the magical skill that Mestre had just shown him. *Nothing's impossible...*

38

A New Brazil

Bernard, Jamie and Rafael arrived outside a brand new building.

Bernard and Rafael took a deep breath as they looked at the construction.

"Are you ready?" Bernard asked, taking Rafael's hand in his.

Rafael nodded his head.

Then they began to walk.

When he'd picked the boys up from the beach, Bernard had explained to Jamie that, before they flew home, there was something they had to do, somewhere they had to go... That it was the reason that he and Rafael had had to come back to Brazil this week.

"But I thought you came back home to watch the Palmeiras match?" Jamie had said.

"No," said Bernard, shaking his head. "We are home for something different. It has taken time to build it, but now we can show you."

As they opened the doors, Jamie thought he saw Rafael and Bernard's eyes glisten with emotion. Then all three of them walked inside.

As soon as they entered, Jamie realized that this was not just any old building. It was a gym, housing a completely new football court. The floor was so clean, it was evident that no one had ever played on it.

After a few minutes, streams of people began to arrive. Each one of them came to give both Rafael and Bernard a hug and then take their place, standing all around the football court.

Soon, the hall was almost entirely full, and it included all the faces that Jamie had seen during his time in Brazil – even the kids from the street were there.

It was strange because it looked as if this was some kind of celebration … and yet not one person was smiling. In Brazil, as Jamie was beginning to find out, this was highly unusual.

It was only when Rafael strode forward into the centre of the court that Jamie began to have some idea what this was all about.

Rafael's hand was visibly trembling as he pulled the cord to separate the drapes which were covering a plaque that had been set into the wall.

Even though he didn't understand all the words, Jamie caught his breath as he read what had been engraved on the plaque.

Para Stephania da Cruz
Ela acreditava que o esporte pode
construir um novo Brasil
De Bernard E Rafael

After he had unveiled the plaque, Rafael took out a piece of paper, cleared his throat and began reading. Or at least he tried. His stutter was so bad and he was so emotional that after a few seconds, Bernard went to join him and together they began speaking, Bernard pausing each time his son stuttered so that they could complete the words in unison.

Jamie felt as though he might cry. He could see how upset Rafael was. Then he felt someone's presence next to him. It was Rosária. She and Mestre had just arrived.

"They are talking about Rafael's mum," she explained. "She was a psychologist and she worked with lots of children all around our city. Rich and poor kids. Everyone. She always said that sport was a way to heal the mind and she believed that all the kids should have somewhere to play together and so ... that is what Bernard and Rafael have built. This is for her. This was her dream."

Jamie nodded. He looked at Rafael and Bernard, who were standing next to each other, holding each other's hands, bravely fighting back the tears.

Jamie felt a tear of his own run down his cheek. He remembered how one day Rafael had tried to describe to him how it felt to have a stutter.

When you stutter, trying to get the word out is like reaching for something that is always out of your grasp, he'd said. It seemed to Jamie that the saddest part of all was that Stephania da Cruz could not help the one boy who really needed her most.

Jamie wiped away the tear and tried to reach for a smile.

"What does the sign say?" he asked Rosária.

"In English, it says *For Stephania da Cruz – She believed sport could build a new Brazil...*"

39

Caneta

Jamie looked at the small, thin boy with something between anger and respect.

This small, thin boy was the same kid, wearing the old, faded Brazil top, that Jamie had seen playing in the slums every day ... and always wearing that same top.

Now they were playing against one another in the first-ever game of futsal in the new Stephania da Cruz gym.

After Bernard made his own speech and the gym was officially opened, all of the kids present – some from the beach, some from the slums and some from the richer suburbs – were invited to take part.

And it had just so happened that Jamie had the misfortune to have been placed on the other side to the boy in the Brazil top ... because that boy had nutmegged him, on purpose, three times already during the game.

Now, he was standing, looking at Jamie, with the cheekiest, most mischievous grin possible.

Not that the kid was Jamie's only problem. This was futsal, not football, and even though Mike's booklet had told him about the smaller ball and goal, it hadn't prepared him for the level of speed and skill this game was played at. Everything seemed to be happening at a hundred miles an hour. Jamie felt dizzy with the intensity of the action.

Time and again, when he had the ball, he was taking too long and being caught in possession. Then, when the other team launched their rapid counter-attacks, Jamie was either out of the game or, worse still, nutmegged by the little boy from the streets.

Finally, to make Jamie's embarrassment complete, not only was he playing on the same side as Rosária – and feeling thoroughly frustrated by his inability to impress her – but he was also aware that Mestre was among the big crowd of Brazilian people watching the game.

Seeing Mestre had given Jamie an idea, though. Perhaps there was *one* way he could show the people watching how good he was.

"*Sim!*" Jamie shouted, remembering Mike's piece of advice to him in his booklet.

Rosária had just collected the ball and turned past a player to get herself an inch of space. Without looking up, Rosária knew it was Jamie's shout and provided him with an instant pass.

Controlling the ball on his thigh, Jamie knew this was the moment to try it. He flicked the ball into the air and began attempting to softly head the ball to himself as he ran forward.

It was a brave move.

And Jamie's attempted A Mágica was over after approximately a second.

He tripped himself up and fell flat on his face, allowing the opposition to score straight away.

The crowd on the touchline could not help but laugh and point at Mestre. They all knew A Mágica was his trademark move and that no one else could replicate it.

Jamie sat, embarrassed, on the floor of the gym. But he was no quitter; he accepted Rosária's firm hand of support and got back up to his feet.

As he jogged into his position waiting for the game to restart, Jamie ran past Mestre. He couldn't help but notice that Mestre was staring straight at him with the exact same look that he had given Jamie on that first morning at the beach. He was focusing angrily at Jamie's trainers.

Jamie could almost hear Mestre talking to him.

You must touch the ball with your feet... Football ... starts with the foot...

Hurriedly, Jamie took off his trainers and his socks to reveal his bare feet. Then he looked again at Mestre.

Mestre was now smiling ... and so was Rosária.

Just as when they had danced at the beach, it was Rosária who was about to lead Jamie ... to show him the way. Except this time she used her skill.

With the ball back in play and with Rosária in possession, one of the opposition players approached her to try and make a tackle. Rosária drew him towards her, dragging the ball back towards her own body using the sole of her foot – and then, as soon as the player got too close, she flicked the ball up and over his head, dancing around the other side, to meet the ball on the drop with a spellbinding volley, which dipped right into the top corner of the goal.

The skill was mesmerizing, and Jamie could not help but applaud. He was in awe of Rosária. He wanted to play like that.

"We are inside but we can still play as if we are by

the sea," she said, giving Jamie a high five. "No matter where you are or who you play against, you can still play with the rhythm and the joy. It's time for you to bring the beach skills back ... OK?"

⑩ Time to Dance

With Rosária's words still ringing in his ear, Jamie closed his eyes. For just one second, he had to shut off everything else in the world. He had to find the beat inside him.

He felt his heart pumping and he listened to its rhythm. Jamie's heart beat for football.

The next time he received the ball, Jamie produced a double drag-back with his first two touches.

"*Olé!*" the crowd shouted.

Then Jamie nutmegged his very next opponent.

"*Caneta!*" "*Ginga!*" the spectators clapped.

Jamie could feel his cheeks burning with pride. He had produced a *caneta*, in Brazil, and, even better, he realized that the player he had nutmegged had been the cheeky little boy with the Brazilian top!

Jamie had nutmegged the tiny prince of the nutmegs!

Now Jamie was starting to get respect. All of his different attributes as a footballer were starting to come to the fore. He had the sure touch from the beach ... he had the extra fitness that running on the sand every day had given him ... he was picking up futsal's quickness of movement and cheeky flicks ... and on top of that, he still retained what he had always had – his trademark rocket-like pace and a fiery determination to never give up, to keep going for every second of the game.

It was a unique combination and, when all of these qualities came together, it meant that Jamie was almost impossible to stop.

"*Ginga!*" the crowd shouted again and again as Jamie began beating players at will. The more they shouted, the more confident he became. They were shouting another word at him too. It began with F and seemed to end with O. Jamie could not quite make it out... But he didn't care. They could shout whatever they wanted. Right now, it was all about the game.

Starting to believe that they quite possibly had a very special player on their side, all of his teammates began giving the ball to Jamie whenever they could ... and now he could see Rosária preparing to flick another pass his way.

Instantly, Jamie controlled the ball on his chest, deftly flicked it past a player using his thigh, and then knocked it down the line to use his pace.

He scorched past the defender and, from a wide angle, took on an audacious curling shot. However, rather than using his instep, Jamie went with the outside of his bare left foot, aiming to curl the ball towards the far corner. The ball started off way outside the line of the far post but, with the amount of extra spin he had been able to generate on the ball by using the outside of his foot, it started to come back in, curling more and more the longer it spent in the air.

The goalkeeper dived high and wide, using all his elasticity to reach the ball, but there was never going be any chance ... Jamie's shot had been destined to nestle in the top corner of the net from the moment he had struck it.

It flew in. *Goooooooool!* Jamie shouted wildly in his head.

It was a phenomenal strike and Jamie raised his hands in the air to take the applause. He even produced something that resembled a little Brazilian samba dance!

Again the crowd clapped; again they shouted that strange word beginning with F at Jamie. Now it seemed everyone was talking about the pale British boy with the colourful Brazilian skills.

In the middle of the spectators, even Mestre was impressed by what he had seen.

He put his hand on Rafael's shoulder, wagged his finger and said with a coach's pride:

"I knew the boy was ready."

At the end of the game, Jamie shook hands with every player on the court. He even got a hug and two kisses on the cheek from Rosária, who actually seemed sad that he was leaving.

Jamie was still pinching himself when the thin boy in the Brazilian shirt came up to him. During the game, he and Jamie had had a titanic battle of nutmegs. He'd done Jamie five times and Jamie had done him twice – and all the while the boy had never stopped smiling.

They did a high five, and although language was a problem, their mutual respect of each other's talent broke through the barrier.

Then the boy began tugging at Jamie's shirt again. Just as he had on Jamie's first day in Brazil.

Jamie looked down at his Hawkstone shirt. He thought long and hard. Then he had an idea.

Jamie pointed to boy's Brazil top. The top was tiny, faded, tattered and ripped … but it was a Brazil football shirt … from the streets of Brazil.

There and then, both boys took off their shirts and swapped. As he handed over his Hawkstone top, for a second Jamie wondered whether Mike would mind – it had been his birthday present, after all – but somewhere in his head he could see Mike smiling proudly. He had a warm feeling in his stomach that told him he was doing exactly the right thing.

Although it was extremely tight on him, Jamie put on his Brazil shirt and walked off the brand new futsal court. He cast his mind forward and imagined the future. Instead of having to play in the stony, dusty, dirty streets, every one of the kids from around the neighbourhood – rich and poor – would all be able to play here, whenever they wanted.

Jamie hoped that, looking down from somewhere, Stephania da Cruz would be very proud.

(41)

Fire in Your Feet

Jamie slid down the window and breathed in the smooth Brazilian night air. Would he ever come back? Would anyone here remember the British boy who came over to play with the Brazilians? Certainly, Jamie would never forget them.

"Hey!" said Jamie, suddenly remembering what he'd been meaning to ask since the game earlier. "You know when we were playing? Every time I got the ball and went on a dribble, all the people watching started shouting something – I think it began with F. Do you know what it was?"

"*Foguinho* is what they were calling you," Bernard answered from the driver's seat. "It is their nickname for you."

For a second the car went silent. The bright lights of the airport loomed into sight just ahead of them. And then it clicked for Jamie.

"What? You mean I have a Brazilian nickname?!" he shouted at such volume that Bernard almost crashed the car. "*I* have a Brazilian nickname! Me, *Jamie Johnson*, has a *Brazilian* nickname! Oh my God! That's amazing!! Wait till I tell Mike and Jack! *Foguinho* … *Foguinho*!! I love it!! Hi, I'm Jamie Johnson … but you can call me *Foguinho*!"

"D-d-on't you w-want to know what it means?" asked Rafael, looking at his friend, who appeared to have gone slightly mad, just repeating the word Foguinho over and over again.

"It means something too?!" yelled Jamie. "Oh, that's even better. This just keeps getting better!! Yes, please tell me! What does my nickname mean?"

"It m-means L-Little Fire."

"Little Fire!! How cool is that? Little Fire – I love it! Is that because I'm small and fast and I burn past the defenders?" asked Jamie.

"Y-y-y-es, p-p-robably," smiled Rafael, who was laughing now. "And m-m-aybe also b-b-because of this!"

Rafael pointed to Jamie's bright red hair.

"Y-y-ou h-have f-f-fire in your f-f-eet, f-f-ire in your heart and f-f-ire on your head!"

"Yeah," laughed Jamie. "Fair point!"

Then, with his excitement at its peak, and, despite the fact that he had never done it before in his life, Jamie suddenly burst into a rap.

"Foguinho is my name,
Football is my game,
I'll take you on, down the line,
I'll skill you up, each and every time!

Don't try to stop me,
Don't even try to foul me,
It makes no difference, how many men surround me.

I'll skill you up,
I'll burn you down,
My. Name. Is. Foguinho.
Little Fire just came to town!"

42

Heading Home

Jamie scratched his scalp and looked at his fingernails. They were full of sand. Normally that might have been a bit disgusting, but, right now, Jamie looked at it a different way. He liked the idea that he was bringing some of Brazil back home in, or rather on, his head.

It wasn't all he'd be bringing back either. He had the skills from Brazil inside him now and he was determined to keep them and practise them every day before the big match at the end of term. When the day came, he wanted to be *ready*, Jamie thought, borrowing the phrase that Mestre always seemed to use.

He smiled to himself and looked at Rafael. His friend

was leaning his head against the aeroplane window with his mouth wide open and his tongue hanging out to the side. Jamie couldn't believe that he had slept for practically the whole flight home.

What made it even more frustrating was that Rafael had promised to tell Jamie the true story of Mestre on the plane – who he really was and how he really got those skills – and then, as soon as they'd eaten their meal, he had fallen fast asleep!

Jamie thought about his time with Mestre. He thought about Rosária and the other kids on the beach and he thought about the amazing night that Bernard had taken Jamie and Rafael to see Palmeiras play. Jamie now understood that, all the time they were there, Bernard had been preparing for the opening of the futsal hall and yet he'd still made time to be the best host for Jamie.

Jamie looked across at Bernard, who was making some architectural sketches, his face as serious as ever.

Jamie undid his seatbelt, stood up and walked over to him.

"Thank you so much for inviting me," said Jamie. "I just hope I didn't disappoint you."

Bernard put down his pencil. "Disappoint me? How?"

"Part of the reason you invited me was to help

Rafa get over his stammer in public and ... it hasn't happened..."

Bernard shook his head. "Jamie, we invited you because you are a true friend to Rafa," he said. "I didn't expect you to cure him. Just to have fun with him. And I know you two did that."

Jamie nodded. "It was the best time of my entire life," he said. "And I'm so sorry about your mirror!"

Bernard didn't respond. Instead, he did something that no man apart from Mike had done to Jamie since his dad had left.

He gave Jamie a hug.

Part
Three

(43)

Talking Tactics

**Wednesday 16 July –
six and a half weeks later –
the day before the game...**

"You need to know your opposition," Mike said, staring at the three young, hopeful faces in front of him. "So what Rafael has been doing: watching the teachers train, working out their formation ... that is exactly the right thing to do."

Jamie, Jack and Rafael looked at one another and smiled. For weeks now, everything they had done had been geared towards this game. As soon as school restarted, Jamie, Jack and Rafael had held trials to see which three players would be joining Jamie and Jack in the side.

There had been lots of good players – both boys and girls – and as captain, Jamie found the process of telling the other kids that they hadn't made it into the team very difficult. In the end, though, Rafael, put it best when he'd said: "You can't make an omelette without breaking some eggs."

And so, finally, the trio had settled on the following team and formation: Jack in goal, the Talbot twins in defence, Aaron Cody in midfield and Jamie in attack.

Not only was Rafael present at every one of the kids' training sessions in the park – always kneeling by the side of the pitch, making notes in his pad and passing on information and tactics to the team via Jamie – he also made sure he saw all of the teachers' training sessions in the playground too. He would conceal himself from Pratley's view by hiding behind the cars and memorizing everything that he saw. He compiled comprehensive fact-files on every member of the teachers' team, all the while devising his own set of special tactics to beat them.

Ultimately, Rafael's tactics revolved around one simple idea: the teachers were playing with Mr Duggins in defence. He was quite a fat man and an extremely slow runner; Mr Pratley had been forced to pick him when Ms Vetterlein had repeated her insistence that she couldn't play in the Teachers v Pupils match because of the Cup Final she was due to play in for Hawkstone the following weekend.

Once news of this had leaked, Rafael had pounced on Duggins' presence in defence as the teachers' weak point and decided that the pupils should attack this weak point with their own strongest, most dangerous threat: Jamie.

Rafael knew that if, whenever he received the ball, Jamie took on Duggins, he would beat him every time. It would unlock the defence. It would unlock the whole game.

If Jamie was the most powerful weapon on the pitch, Rafael was the mastermind off it. He had told every player of their individual responsibilities and they all knew the overall team tactics off by heart. All the work had been done. Everything was set and now, the night before the game itself, Jamie, Jack and Rafael had come to see the man who knew more about winning big matches than all of them put together. Mike Johnson.

"Have your tactics but also be prepared to change," Mike told them. "A match evolves during its course. It never stays the same. If you are too regimented – just sticking to your original plan – you will break. You have to be flexible to change with the circumstances."

While Jamie and Jack listened intently, Rafael nodded and wrote furiously into his notepad. He soaked up every piece of football information that was ever offered to him.

"And above all, if you defeat your opponents, never gloat. The time of your greatest triumph is the time to show some humility ... and that goes for life as well as football."

Mike took a big gulp of coffee and let his words sink in.

"Good luck, you lot," he said. "Go and make it happen."

(44) The Truth of the Legend

Jamie walked home that night with an extra spring in his step.

After they left Mike's, he, Jack and Rafael had had a group hug. They knew that the next time they would all see one another would be the day of the game itself. The day they hoped to lift that gleaming school trophy.

And Jamie knew that he was ready.

Everything about the way his body felt told him so. Not just because he had been training with Jack and the rest of the team every afternoon, carefully keeping to Rafael's set plan and tactics, but also because, even after he left them, every night he'd been continuing his own search for footballing perfection.

Taking his mind back to Brazil, he had devoted countless hours working on every single skill that he had learned over there. While he practised, he imagined Mestre standing – arms folded – nodding occasionally, guiding Jamie in the art and skill of Brazilian brilliance. Once, when attempting A Mágica, he'd even managed to walk a few steps with the ball balancing on his head! He'd called Rafael straight away to see if he could somehow get the message back to Mestre in Brazil!

Jamie was surprised at how often he had thought of Mestre since they had got home. His presence seemed to be with Jamie all the time. Perhaps it was because of the story of his life. Rafael had finally told Jamie the truth about Mestre the day after they had got back home from Brazil, and it was a story Jamie could not forget.

"Come on then," Jamie had said to Rafael. "You said it was a good story. And it must be: to get skills like that … to be able to do A Mágica. Go on, tell me; what's the deal with Mestre?"

"Mestre was brought up in the slums, one of the poorest of them all," Rafael had begun. "He was a brilliant young footballer but his family had no money whatsoever and so, like many others, as a young boy, he turned to crime to get by. He pickpocketed people, stole from shops, that kind of thing … but then, when he got older, it became more serious, and when he was nineteen, he was sent to prison for thirteen years.

"In those thirteen years, he was let out for only one hour each day. The rest of the day, it was just him in that cell alone. He had only one possession: a tiny little ping-pong ball. He spent ten hours every day for thirteen years practising his touch with that little ping-pong ball … and it was that little ping-pong ball which gave him all his skills. By the time he was released, it was too late for him to become a footballer, but even though he couldn't be a professional, he now had the touch of a magician. He went to prison a boy, a young criminal. He came out as O Mestre."

"Wow," said Jamie. "That's sad, but it's incredible, and it makes sense too. If you can control a ping-pong ball in a prison cell, no wonder you'll have become a master with a normal ball by the time you get out. That is some story."

"You're right, it is sad," Rafael said. "Because although he now had the touch of a genius, it was too late for him in the professional game. So he did the next best thing: he taught his skills to the kids. And, as you know, he has helped at least one boy go on to be a professional footballer…"

Jamie nodded. He thought about Arnaldo a lot too.

"No wonder you've got so much respect for him," Jamie said. "He's an amazing man."

"True enough," smiled Rafael. "And he has a very pretty daughter!"

Let Down

Thursday 17 July
Match Day: 08.04

"You're not coming, are you?"

Just one look at his mum's face told Jamie everything he needed to know.

"Jamie, they just called me this morning. They're short. They need me."

"I knew it! I knew this was going to happen! Why didn't you just say you weren't going to come in the first place?" he stormed. He wanted her to be there so much. He was so upset, so desperately disappointed ... he just had no way of handling it.

"I wanted to come, Jamie. You know I would love to, but this is my job. I've got no choice. You'll still have Mike there…"

"Exactly!" shouted Jamie. "Because he's the only one that cares about me!"

"Jamie!" his mum pleaded. "Jamie! Wait!"

But he was gone. Slamming the door shut so hard behind him that the whole of their little house shuddered.

"What's wrong with you?" asked Jack, who was waiting for Jamie outside her house. Her excitement for the match had changed to concern as soon as she saw Jamie.

Jamie shrugged and shook his head. He'd been on a high ever since he'd got back from Brazil. He'd felt so relaxed and confident ... probably the happiest he'd ever been. And yet now – on this day of all days – he could only feel anger.

The worst part was that, somewhere in his mind, he'd been expecting this. Whenever he was really looking forward to something, he always got let down in the end.

"Have you got your match kit?" Jack asked.

"Course I do!" snapped Jamie.

Jack stared at him. He never talked to her like this.

"Look!" he shouted, opening his bag for her to see. "Got everything apart from socks and shin pads. Happy now?"

"Don't you want to get your socks and shin pads?"

"Not if it means going back home!" barked Jamie.

The Big Warm-Up

Match Day: 11.07

Aaron Cody, Dexter and Kane Talbot and Jamie Johnson all lined up on the edge of the area to take their shots at goal. Jack Marshall bounced in anticipation between the posts and Rafael da Cruz looked on watchfully from behind the goal.

It was break time and, while they were practising, the rest of the kids were placing chairs around the playground's edge. The whole school would be watching later and lots of parents would too. Everything had to be in place. Very soon, the school trophy would be brought out if its cabinet. That's when things started to get really exciting.

Now it was time for the final warm-up. The last chance to loosen muscles and work on tactics before kick-off, which was just over three hours away.

Jamie could sense the eyes of the other kids on him. It was the same when he watched Hawkstone warm up: he always focused on the star player, Harry Armstrong, analysing his every movement. He knew the other, younger kids were doing that with him right now.

Jamie watched and waited his turn as Aaron Cody coolly slotted his shot home, followed by Dexter Talbot, who blasted his effort into the roof of the net. Kane Talbot was next – he saw his strike brilliantly saved down to the left by Jack Marshall.

And then it was Jamie's go. All the kids putting the chairs down stopped what they were doing in order to watch.

Jamie waited in readiness on the edge of the area as Aaron Cody softly rolled a cross along the ground towards him.

Jamie saw the ball coming. He analysed its speed and direction, gathered all his strength and then went for a major blaster of a strike.

To his and everyone else's horror, he missed the ball entirely. A complete air shot.

"Give us another one," he shouted quickly, before

anyone had a chance to react. "There was something in my eye."

So, from the other side of the pitch, Dexter Talbot spun over a perfect cross. It was a juicy pass, drifting through the air, just begging to be hit.

Jamie saw the ball coming and this time elected to take it on the volley. He swivelled, planted his right foot firmly in the ground, and shaped his body for a left-foot strike. Then he attacked the ball with a violent swipe.

This time he made contact all right … but in the worst possible way. Jamie ballooned the ball – not only over the goal, but also over the whole of the school building.

Everyone watched it sail skywards and then drop into the car park next to the school gates. The ball must have hit the roof of a car because there was an audible thud followed by the loud wail of an alarm going off.

It was not just the car that was alarmed.

Some of the kids gasped. Most were shocked into silence. This was Jamie Johnson. This was the best player in the school. This was three hours before kick-off. This was a major problem.

"What's wrong, JJ?" asked Jack as she and Rafael came to talk to their friend.

"Is it n-nerves? Are y-you OK?" asked Rafael.

Jamie hung his head.

He was anything but OK.

(47)

Quick Getaway

Match Day: 13.32

Everything was set. Just lunch and then kick-off.

"Where you going?" asked Jack. "We need our fuel."

She had been keeping an eye on Jamie today. She could tell he was not right.

And now, just as they were going into lunch, he seemed to be slipping away, going somewhere else.

"Gotta go and do something," was all Jamie would say. "Don't worry. I'll be back for the match."

Jamie waited until everyone had gone for lunch. Then he went into the toilets, took off his shirt and trousers, put on his football gear and put his school clothes back on over the top.

It was a boiling hot day and Jamie now had way too many layers on but he didn't care. All he cared about was that Mike had got the text that he had sent an hour before.

Those two shots Jamie had taken at break time had been horrific. He knew that there was no way he could play in this game while his argument with his mum that morning was still on his mind. He had to make up with her. It was the only way for him to sort himself out. He just hoped Mike would be able to help him.

Jamie walked out of the back exit of the school, checked his watch, checked that no one was looking and then vaulted the school gate as quickly as he could.

He saw the car and sprinted across the road to get in. He checked again. Thankfully, no one had seen him.

Mike Johnson smiled and patted Jamie on the knee.

"I've got to be back in thirty minutes," said Jamie.

Mike smiled and started the car.

"We'll have you back in twenty-five."

Ready for
the Whistle

Match Day: 14.12

The whole school was waiting.

Rafael was going out of his mind, tearing through the pages of his notepad, trying to work out a different tactical plan.

Jack was kicking the goalposts in frustration.

And Mr Pratley was smiling. Just three minutes left until kick-off.

Jamie Johnson had bottled it. He was a no-show.

And then, finally, he appeared.

"What?" Jamie smiled nonchalantly at Jack. "I told you I'd be back for the match!"

Jamie sprinted on to the pitch, in his full kit, missing

only his shin pads and socks, ready to take the kick-off for the pupils' team.

As Mr Karenza made Jamie and Pratley shake hands before the start, Jamie looked around at all the people who were watching: every single pupil and loads of parents too.

Jamie did not have either of his parents there to watch. But that was OK, now that he had made up with his mum.

She had been taken completely by surprise, not just to see Jamie and Mike suddenly appear at the hospital while she was working, but with the massive bunch of flowers they had for her too.

"I just wanted to say I'm sorry, Mum," Jamie had said. "I understand that you can't come to the game because you have to work and I know that the whole reason you work is for me … for us. I was an idiot to shout at you. Will you forgive me, please?"

Jamie's mum had given him the warmest hug in the world.

"Of course I forgive you, Jamie," she'd said.

Jamie had felt the biggest sense of relief. Nothing stressed him out more than arguing with his mum.

"Thank you," he'd smiled. "I really don't think I could have played properly in this match otherwise."

Then Mike had said: "JJ and I have had a little idea,

Karen. We'd like you to ride again. I just called the stables up at Edgemont Farm. Would you believe June Leon is still working there? She says they've got a lovely big horse who's perfect for you. His name is Ivan and she says you can go up there anytime you like."

Jamie's mum had cried a little bit. She'd thanked them and said she would visit the stables that weekend. Then she'd told them to get back to school as quickly as possible. She knew how important this game was.

"Just make sure you score the winning goal for me, Jamie," she'd whispered in her son's ear.

The Plan Comes Together

 The BIG Match
Team Line Ups

Referee: Mr Karenza

Teachers	Pupils
Mr McManus (gk)	Jack Marshall (gk)
Mr Duggins	Dexter Talbot
Mr Glyn	Kane Talbot
Mr Regis	Aaron Cody
Mr Pratley (c)	Jamie Johnson (c)

20 mins per half

Right from the kick-off, Rafael's plan worked to perfection.

Jamie always made sure that he was marked by Mr Duggins and, whenever he got the ball, he simply destroyed him for pace.

The first goal was a perfect example. Dexter Talbot tackled Mr Sagrott and, without a moment's hesitation, slid the ball through to Jamie. Jamie could feel that Mr Duggins was close behind him so he let the ball go past on purpose. Then it was just a straight race between him and Duggins for the ball.

Jamie motored past him, barely having to go into his turbo-gear to ease away. Mr McManus came out of his goal to close down the angles but Jamie just breezed past him too.

He looked around and saw that he was so far clear that he even waited for Mr Duggins to chug back towards his own goal.

Jamie watched Duggins sprinting towards him before, at the very last minute, swerving his body out of the way so Duggins crashed straight into the goalpost. Then Jamie simply walked the ball into the net.

The plan had worked like clockwork. The pupils were ahead within five minutes!

Teachers 0 — 1 Pupils
J Johnson, 4

On the touchline, the kids roared and so did some of their supporters, Mike the loudest among them.

"That's my boy, JJ!" he shouted proudly as Jamie sprinted over to celebrate with him.

"That one's for Garrincha!" yelled Jamie, leaping into the air to give Mike a high five.

Meanwhile, standing just in front of Bernard, Rafael calmly made some extra notes in his pad. The game was unfolding just as he had hoped – but he knew it was still very early days.

Now, with confidence coursing through their side, the pupils started to play some slick one-touch passing football, all with the aim of releasing Jamie when the time was right.

It was Jack who spotted the next opportunity to do so. She slung a quick pass out to Jamie, who controlled the ball softly on his thigh before standing up straight to see which direction Mr Duggins was going to come from.

Immediately, he saw Mr Duggins loping towards him. There was only a second to think, but Jamie smiled because he knew exactly what he was going to do. He waited until Mr Duggins was close enough and then, ever so sneakily, Jamie flicked the ball right between Mr Duggins' legs.

"*Caneta!*" Mike shouted from the sideline, to strange looks from all around.

But Jamie knew what he was talking about – Jamie had just nutmegged a teacher in front of everyone! Mr Duggins tried to turn around but his big wobbly body could not contend with the pace at which Jamie was moving … instead of spinning and chasing after Jamie, Mr Duggins just toppled to the ground.

Jamie sprinted on, flicked the ball into the air and volleyed a pass over to Aaron Cody, who met the centre with a perfect first-time finish. This was the playground of Wheatlands School but it could have been a beach in Brazil!

Now the kids were really starting to understand that this *could happen*…

From somewhere behind one of the goals, a chant began:

"And now you're gonna believe us…
And now you're gonna believe us…
And now you're gonna belieeeeve us…
We're gonna beat the teachers!"

All around the playground the kids were now chanting and singing:

"Pratley! What's the score?
Pratley, Pratley what's the score?"

Jamie punched the air. His team were right on track to create school history and he was now seriously in the mood.

J Johnson, 4
A Cody, 9

"He needs help!" shouted Mr Pratley. He was crouching down beside Mr Duggins and seemed to be whispering something in his ear.

"It's my left — I mean my right knee," Duggins was saying, grimacing as he clutched it. "I fell when Johnson nutmegged me."

"Can you go in goal and give it five minutes?" asked Mr Karenza, now also on the scene. "Maybe it'll get better."

"No," said Mr Duggins, almost before Mr Karenza had finished the question. "I'm afraid I can't continue. I'll need to be substituted."

"Yes, he'll have to be substituted," repeated Mr Pratley now. "He'll have to come off and we'll have to get a replacement."

"But there are no subs," said Mr Karenza. "Who can you get?"

Jamie and Jack, who had now joined the group around Duggins, looked at each other. They knew the answer before Pratley had even said it.

"It has to be Ms Vetterlein," smiled Mr Pratley.

⑤⓪
The Move

"I'm sorry," said Ms Vetterlein apologetically.

She was standing watching the game from the sidelines like the rest of the school.

"But we've got a Cup Final at the weekend and I promised my manager I wouldn't play today."

Jamie and Jack breathed a huge sigh of relief. They had immediately argued that it would be completely unfair if the teachers got Ms Vetterlein – she was a semi-professional, after all.

"Of course you can play," shouted Pratley. "You'll have to."

For a second there was widespread shouting on and off the pitch as all the players, pupils and spectators had their say.

"It you could play, Ms Vetterlein, it really would help us out greatly," said Mr Karenza finally, attempting to restore some order to proceedings. "If the teachers' team don't have enough players then we'll have to abandon the match, which would be such a shame … for everyone."

Ms Vetterlein looked at Pratley and then again at Mr Karenza.

"We'd really appreciate it," Mr Karenza repeated.

"Go on then," she said finally. "What harm can it do? Where do you want me to play, Mr Pratley?"

With that, she jogged athletically on to the pitch. She didn't even have to change because she was already wearing her tracksuit and trainers.

As she joined the game, a cool air of fear swept around the pupils team. Ms Vetterlein was some player. Although she was nice and cheery around school, all the kids had seen her play for Hawkstone ladies'; on the pitch she was a natural-born predator. One chance equalled one goal.

"You go up front," Pratley told Ms Vetterlein. "I'll take care of Johnson at the back."

It was the kind of substitution that could alter the whole face of the game. It was almost as if Pratley had planned the entire thing from the very beginning.

*

Rafael da Cruz sprinted around the pitch to crouch down behind the goal. When he got there, he tore through his pad, searching desperately for other plans … other formations.

The kids just could not deal with Ms Vetterlein's movement. She seemed to have the ability to ghost unmarked into the most dangerous positions. She had Rafael extremely worried … and rightly so.

Three times in the space of seven minutes she worked herself free inside the box, and on each occasion, she finished with the cold touch of an assassin. She struck her first goal to Jack's left, her second to Jack's right and, for her hat-trick, she chipped the ball over Jack's desperate stretch.

Ms Vetterlein had turned the game on its head in what seemed like the flick of a switch.

Teachers 3 — 2 Pupils
H Vetterlein. 10.14.17   J Johnson. 4
A Cody. 9

While Rafael had been wracking his brains for tactical solutions, Pratley had milked all of the goals to their fullest, cheering them loudly right in front of the kids, before leading his teammates in aeroplane-style celebrations.

Watching Pratley's sickening smile as he pranced

around the playground like an overgrown baby had almost made Jamie puke into his own mouth.

Yet that wasn't even the biggest of Jamie's problems. With Ms Vetterlein now up front, Pratley had dropped back into defence to replace Duggins, and he was an entirely different opponent for Jamie to counter.

"Go on," Pratley had said to Jamie during their first one on one. "Knock it past me and then run after it. Kick and chase … but where's your skill?"

Each time Jamie got the ball and prodded it down the line to run after, Pratley always seemed to be there, either anticipating Jamie's run or else fouling him to make sure he couldn't get away. Suddenly, Jamie's threat seemed to have been eradicated.

Then, with half-time fast approaching, Ms Vetterlein went on another direct run right into the heart of the pupils' territory. She twisted both the Talbot twins inside and out, rendering them dizzy and bewildered, before somehow finding a powerfully accurate shot from the acutest of angles.

Before anyone could react, the ball was in the back of the net once more.

"Ha ha ha!!!" screamed Pratley, joyously. "This is too easy!"

Mr Karenza blew his whistle. "4–2 to the teachers," he announced. "And that's half-time!"

"No goal!" shouted Jack, suddenly rushing out from her area to confront Mr Karenza. She had a mixture of anger and panic etched on her face. "Sir! The ball went in through the side-netting – it's no goal!"

"Oh, be quiet, Marshall!" said Pratley. "Stop being such a bad loser!"

Pratley bounced up to Ms Vetterlein to give her a high five.

"Put it there, partner!" he shouted, cheesily.

However, Ms Vetterlein left Pratley hanging.

"She's right, Mr Karenza," said Ms Vetterlein. "It went in through that hole in the side netting. The goal shouldn't stand."

"Whaaaat!" screamed Pratley at his teammate. "What are you doing?!"

Mr Karenza looked at the little gap in the side of the net. Then he looked again at Ms Vetterlein for a second before blowing his whistle.

"My mistake," he shouted. "That was no goal. The score remains 3–2 and that *is* half-time!"

51

How Do We Stop Vetterlein?

HALF-TIME
Teachers 3   –   2 Pupils
H Vetterlein, 10,14,17   J Johnson, 4
                             A Cody, 9

"Come on, guys!" said Jamie, looking at each one of his teammates individually. "We're only one down – and we could have been two down! This is the exact time we have to step it up. We have to fight harder, run faster and play even better.

"If we want this – if we want to be the first pupils team to win this game – the next twenty minutes have to be the best football we've ever played! We can do this!"

220

Jamie bit into his orange and tried to keep his body calm. Had he said enough? Had he inspired his teammates to make a comeback? Could they stop the teachers now that they had Ms Vetterlein?

Jamie watched his teammates nod back at him. They were supporting him as their captain; they were behind him. But they also needed more. They needed a plan.

"Rafael," said Jamie. "How do we do it?"

The plan was clear and concise. Rafael said that, with Vetterlein now on the pitch, it left them far too exposed at the back. They had to revert to a more defensive formation. They would switch to three men at the back with just Jamie in midfield. He even instructed Dexter and Kane Talbot to both man-to-man mark Ms Vetterlein.

McManus

Pratley   Glyn

Regis   Johnson

Cody

Talbot (K)   Vetterlein
                    Talbot (D)

Marshall

RDC

Even through his stutter, everyone clearly understood their role. Rafael was still fluent in football.

"This whole plan relies on you and your discipline," Rafael said privately to Jamie just before the re-start.

"THE most important thing is that, when we don't have the ball, *you hold*," he warned. "You have to keep your defensive position, Jamie, because if you if you leave that position … you are out of the game and our whole plan is destroyed."

⑤② Taking the Bait

The tactics worked. Playing three at the back with both Talbot twins marking and Jamie cutting off the supply line in the midfield starved Vetterlein of the ammunition she required.

Yet it also meant that the pupils had no attacking threat themselves. On the rare occasions that Jamie even got the ball, he was so isOláted that he had to try and take on all the teachers by himself. It was impossible.

All the while, the minutes were still ticking by … and the pupils were still losing 3–2.

Then with four minutes left to go, Pratley, who was in possession of the ball, did something very unusual. He did nothing. Nothing at all.

He did not try a pass or a dribble. He did not attempt a shot. He just stood, with his foot resting on top of the ball, waiting…

Jamie looked at Rafael.

"HOLD," Rafael mouthed urgently.

"3–2 to us, isn't it, Johnson?" Pratley asked. "So we don't have to attack. You have to come and get it."

With that, Pratley just started doing kick-ups and whistling.

"Boooooooo!" jeered all the kids on the sidelines. "Time-waster!!!"

But Pratley didn't care. He knew his team just had to keep hold of the ball for three more minutes and the game would be over.

Jamie could feel his cold fury starting to boil into hot anger.

He knew Rafael was still mouthing that he should *hold*, that he should stay in position, but it was no use. The more Jamie looked at Pratley's smarmy face and heard his stupid whistling the more the rage was growing. Then the cord snapped.

Jamie left his holding position in the midfield and tore up the pitch at rocket speed, straight towards Pratley.

This was exactly what Pratley had been waiting for. With Jamie now having vacated the midfield space,

Pratley immediately clicked into action, playing a quick one–two with Ms Vetterlein. Then he dashed into the gap that Jamie had left behind.

Jamie watched in horror as Pratley advanced towards the goal and drew back his foot to strike.

Jamie knew if Pratley scored, it would all be his fault. He couldn't let this happen.

Just as Pratley was about to shoot the ball home, Jamie flew into the air and took him down from behind. He'd had no other option.

Mr Karenza blew his whistle hard and loud. Meanwhile Pratley just lay on the ground. It was so obvious, he hadn't even had to claim a penalty.

Then he slowly stood up with a huge satisfied smile on his face. Jamie Johnson had fallen into his trap. He'd taken the bait.

Mr Karenza picked up the ball and walked over to Jamie. "I'm not going to end the year with a sending-off – this is *supposed* to be a friendly game, Jamie ... so that is a yellow card for you," he said.

Then Mr Karenza raised his voice for everyone to hear.

"Penalty for the teachers," he shouted. "Two minutes left to go!"

53

The Penalty

"I'm taking this one!" said Pratley, snatching the ball from Ms Vetterlein.

"Are you sure?" she said calmly. "You do know I've never mis—"

"Of course I'm sure," he snorted. "You've had your goals. This one's mine."

With that, he placed the ball down on the spot and took four deliberate, slow steps backwards. Then he walked back to the ball, picked it up and replaced it in exactly the same position.

"Booo!" shouted all the kids watching the game. "He's time-wasting, Ref!!"

"Better hurry it up a little, please, Colin," said Mr Karenza, blowing his whistle again.

Jamie prayed to all the gods of football as he watched Jack jumping around on the spot, springing into the air to prepare herself to face Pratley's penalty.

Everything is riding on this one moment, Jamie thought. *Please – let her do this...*

Then it went deadly quiet as everyone in the school saw Mr Pratley stride purposefully towards the goal. It was this to win it.

Colin Pratley readied himself, took aim and then fired. He thumped the ball as hard as he was able, sending it shooting through the air, heading straight for the top corner of the net.

"Goal!" he shouted as soon as the ball left his foot.

However, Mr Pratley did not have any idea quite how good a goalkeeper Jacqueline Marshall really was.

Jack flew into the air like an eagle, stretching every muscle and sinew of her body towards the ball. She reached out her hand and, with the very tip of her finger, clawed the speeding ball on to the post.

"Woooaaah!" reacted the crowd as they saw the ball rebound from the post and roll along the goal-line before Jack leapt across to smother it.

"Yes!" shouted Jamie, sprinting over to Jack and giving her a massive high five. "That was blinding!! You saved it! And you saved me – if they'd have scored, it would have been completely my fault!"

"What did you expect?" said Jack, laughing. "Now get upfield, will you? There's only a few seconds left!"

Teachers 3   –   2 Pupils
H Vetterlein, 10,14, 17   J Johnson, 4
A Cody, 9

---

17 seconds remaining

Aaron Cody tried one final, long, desperate pass out to Jamie on the wing. He had overhit it, though, and the ball was flying frustratingly out of play behind the teachers' goal.

Aaron Cody dropped his head. So too did the Talbot Twins, Jack Marshall, Rafael, Bernard, Mike and everyone else who wanted the kids to win. They all knew that, once the ball went out of play, Mr McManus only had to do a little time-wasting with the resulting goal-kick and it would all be over.

The same result as always: the teachers beating the pupils...

However, one of the kids was thinking of something else, somewhere entirely different. Seeing the ball loop past him, Jamie's mind reverted to the beach ... to playing Keepy Uppy with the rest of Mestre's skills students by the water's edge.

What would he have done had he still been there?

How would he have reacted to the ball threatening to get away from him?

Jamie's body answered the question before his mind. He raced after the flying ball, dashing across the hard playground cement just as if he were scampering across the boiling hot sand towards the soothing cool blue sea.

Jamie knew that the only way he could keep the ball alive was to meet it … in the air…

He launched himself towards the ball and, in mid-air, somehow managed to produce a perfect bicycle kick to not only keep the ball in play but also volley it hard and fast back across the goal.

The ball scorched through the air, crashing smack into the back of Pratley's head, rebounding directly towards the goal at unstoppable speed. Mr McManus was motionless as the ball bulleted past him. Pratley, with a little help from Jamie's bicycle kick, had produced the perfect goalscoring header. The only problem for him was that it was an own goal.

"Yessss!" roared Jamie, pumping his fist.

"Noooo!" wailed Pratley.

"Full time!" announced Mr Karenza.

FULL-TIME

Teachers 3   –   3 Pupils

H Vetterlein, 10,14, 17

J Johnson, 4

A Cody, 9

C Pratley, 39 (06)

54

All Over?

It may have been full time but that did not mean that this game was over. Not just yet.

"OK," said Mr Karenza, looking at his watch. "The match is drawn 3–3, but we need to have a winner in this game, so ... now we'll play next goal wins!"

Mr Karenza blew his whistle to restart the game.

Jamie stood bent over with his hands on his thighs, panting. He had given everything in this game; every ounce of energy that every cell in his body had to offer.

He was also paying the price for the fact that they were playing on hard playground cement rather than soft beach sand. He looked down and saw the cuts, grazes and gashes that now made his left leg look like something from a horror movie.

He had given his all. He had nothing left.

And then the chant started.

Softly at first, but getting louder and louder.

"*One Jamie Johnson,*" the kids started to sing. "*There's only one Jamie Johhhhnsonn.*"

Jamie looked at all the kids in the school. He knew how desperately they wanted to win this game; how much they wanted to put one over on the teachers ... how they yearned for this victory.

Then Jamie looked at Mike. He was singing too. In fact, Jamie would have put money on the fact that it was Mike who had started the Jamie Johnson song in the first place.

"*One Jamie Johnson!*" his grandfather was bellowing.

"*There's only one Jamie Johnsooooon!*"

First Jamie felt the buzz. Then his heart started to pump a little faster. He sensed the strength start to flood back into his body and felt the skills coming through, ready to shine.

He was ready for one last push.

Jamie immediately called for the ball and sprinted straight at Pratley. He felt so strong and confident ... and cheeky.

With futsal-like speed, he flicked the ball between Pratley's legs for his second nutmeg of the game and was just about to run through for a shot on goal when Pratley pulled him back by his shirt.

But Mr Karenza waved play on. He hadn't seen it.

The force was with Jamie now. He was motoring. He felt good but, on each occasion that he threatened to get away, Pratley simply did the same thing – he tugged Jamie back by the shirt.

Finally, on the third occasion, Mr Karenza intervened.

"That's a booking for you I'm afraid, Mr Pratley," he said almost apologetically.

"About time!" snapped Jamie. "He keeps pulling my shirt – if he does it again you've got to send him off!"

At this outburst, Pratley and Mr Karenza immediately turned their attention to Jamie, both frowning at him with an expression that suggested Jamie had overstepped the mark.

"You've got a short memory, Jamie!" said Mr Karenza.

He was referring to the foul that Jamie had committed for the penalty. And he had a point; Jamie was lucky to still be on the pitch himself.

What was more, given the fact that Mr Karenza had already said that he didn't want to send anyone off today, it was difficult to imagine that he would now send off one of his own teachers.

But what did that mean? That Pratley had free rein to keep pulling Jamie's shirt for the rest of the match? If that was the case, then Jamie was finished.

Jamie looked across to Mike in despair. As always, Mike's demeanour was calm and positive. He pointed to his head and told Jamie to think.

And that was exactly what Jamie did. He searched his mind for an answer; for a solution that would allow him to get away from Pratley – even if it was just once. Quickly, he dug deep into the depths of his brain until he saw a small chink of light.

Without saying a word to anyone, Jamie reached his arms over his shoulders and pulled off his top, chucking it to the ground by the side of the pitch.

The people watching the game looked at Jamie. Some thought he had taken off his shirt as an act of disgust at Pratley's constant fouling. Others believed it was because of the heat.

They were wrong.

Jamie had taken off his shirt because he wanted to expose the top he had on underneath.

The item of clothing he now displayed to everyone

was very old. It was dirty too. It had holes in it and it was so tight Jamie could barely breathe. And that was exactly the point ... it was so tight that Pratley would never be able to tug his shirt in a million years, even if he tried – there just wasn't enough material.

Jamie looked down at his faded old Brazil shirt and thought back to the first time that he had seen it: when the kids playing in the slum had rushed towards him and when he had looked into the small, thin boy's eyes for the first time.

Meanwhile, on the sidelines, Rafael had also noted Jamie's change of clothing and it had given him his own idea.

It was in the middle of the game and the ball was in play but Rafael quickly called Jamie over to talk to him; to give him one final, vital message ... in the form of two crucial words.

He whispered those two words into Jarnie's ear, only for Jamie to turn and look at him as though he were beyond mad.

"What are you doing?!" the kids shouted anxiously, aware that, with Jamie off the pitch, their team was down to four players and Vetterlein could score the golden goal at any moment. "Jamie! Get back on!"

Jamie was still looking questioningly at Rafael and

the two words he had said. Doubt was etched across his face.

But the link between the two boys was now like that between a top coach and a star player. Rafael knew exactly what to say to Jamie and when.

Rafael nodded to Jamie and mouthed six more words:

Do it, Jamie. You are ready.

This time Jamie nodded back.

55

Ginga!

Jamie flicked the ball into the air and drew all of his skill, rhythm and passion into one place. Then he tilted his head back and bounced the ball on his forehead.

Next, continuing to bounce the ball on his head, Jamie did what he did best. He ran.

Heading the ball in the air as he ran, Jamie skipped past one, two, three of the teachers, who were unable to even attempt a tackle on Jamie because the ball wasn't on the ground for them to contest.

Jamie smiled. He was actually doing it. If only Mestre could see him now.

"Wowwwww!" shouted the kids.

"The boy's a genius," said Mike, shaking his head in

disbelief at what his grandson was managing to achieve.

The only person in the whole playground who was not shocked by what Jamie was doing was Rafael da Cruz. After all, it had been his suggestion.

Jamie had followed Rafael's instruction and he was proving his friend right with each step that he took. There was now only Pratley left to beat. Jamie ran on, confident that with the ball on his head and his Brazil top too tight to pull, Pratley had no possible way of stopping him.

Jamie remembered how Pratley had doubted his ability earlier in the term and how much it had hurt him.

Ginga! Jamie roared in his head as a danced past Pratley. *That's what I have that other players don't: ging—*

Jamie suddenly felt a sharp stab of pain spear into the back of his left foot. Before he could turn to see what it was, he was tumbling helplessly, face first, into the ground.

To gasps of shock and concern from the crowd, Jamie smacked his chin with dangerous force directly on to the cement and immediately sensed the warm trickle of blood ooze from the wound.

Very quickly, he understood what had happened: Pratley hadn't been able to tug his shirt, so, instead, he'd trodden on Jamie's heel as he'd gone past.

Jamie was now lying stricken on the ground, with a hole in his chin and no trainer on his left foot.

It was over.

Or at least it would have been for any other player.

Jamie was back up in a millisecond, running, with one of his feet completely bare on the rough concrete ground. And yet he felt no pain whatsoever; the hardened outer layer of skin on the sole of his foot was protecting him completely.

He latched back on to the loose ball and touched it once, softly, with his instep. Then, without a second's extra thought, he let go of his strike.

The ball flew off the outside of Jamie's bare left foot, swerving and curling deliciously in the air before bending back in to crash home off the inside of the far post.

Jamie went blank. Everything went silent.

Then, with a rush of noise and with his teammates piling all over him, the world returned.

FINAL SCORE
Teachers 3   –   4 Pupils (after extra time)
H Vetterlein, 10,14, 17   J Johnson, 4, 46
                          A Cody, 9
                          C Pratley, 39 (OG)

Pupils win Wheatlands School Cup
for the first time

56

Championes, Championes, Olé, Olé, Olé!

"Well, well, well," said Mr Karenza.

He was holding a microphone so all the kids, teachers and parents could hear what he was saying. He and the two teams were standing in the middle of the playground, with everyone else watching in a huge circle around them.

"We started this game up eleven years ago because we thought that, as the Year 6s prepared to head to their next school, it would be a fun opportunity for them to show their abilities and to go up against the teachers. Well, we obviously had no idea what we were starting!"

The parents all laughed at this comment.

"Each year, the event has grown and the game has got more competitive and, as you know, this is the very first year that the pupils have won."

All the kids and the parents in the crowd cheered.

"So we wish all of Year 6 the best of luck in your new schools and, remember, you can all take what has happened today as a lesson: just because something has never been done before, doesn't mean that it's impossible.

"So our congratulations and the trophy go to the pupils and their captain, Jamie Johnson. If you'd like to come and lift the trophy, Jamie."

A huge roar went up around the playground as Jamie, a little embarrassed at all the attention, walked forward. He wiped his sweaty palms on his old Brazil top and shook hands with Mr Karenza.

Then he placed his hands on the gleaming trophy. This was the first real trophy he had ever won. It was the trophy he had dreamed about lifting for months.

But he knew he could not lift it alone.

"Come on, guys," he shouted to his teammates. "And you too, Rafa! Come and lift it with me!"

It was only when they were all there, all with their hands on the trophy and with all the kids in the playground making the noise of a drumroll, that Jamie and his team finally lifted the prize high into the air.

They were the champions. At last.

57

The Gift

"I still don't know how we lost it!" Colin Pratley was saying, shaking his head.

He was sitting down by one of the goals, talking to, or rather at, Gerald Duggins – the only person who was prepared to listen.

The game had finished ten minutes before, and since then, the playground had been turned into party central! Jamie, Jack, Rafael, the Talbot Twins and Aaron Cody had all been lifted up into the air and given the bumps by the other kids.

Then Rafael started playing samba music through his phone and he and Jamie showed everyone how to dance Brazilian style ... even Mike had joined in. After all, that was his dream: to watch some Brazilian football skills and then dance the samba afterwards. Now he was even dancing with Ms Vetterlein!

The only person who was not enjoying himself was Colin Pratley. Not only had he lost the big match but Mr Karenza had just announced that the teachers would have a new captain for next year. It was odds-on to be Ms Vetterlein.

"Johnson should have been sent off when he brought me down for the penalty," Pratley moaned, continuing his rant to Mr Duggins, who was nodding obediently.

"He shouldn't have even been on the pitch to score the winner ... and what was that *thing* he was doing bouncing the ball on his head anyway? How are we even supposed to stop that?"

"You can't," said Rafael da Cruz, breaking away from the celebrations. He was standing looking down at Pratley. "That's the whole point."

For a second, Pratley was speechless – stunned by Rafael's confidence. It was Rafael's special tactics that had won the game for the pupils. He was now speaking with the confidence of a champion.

"It's called A Mágica," Rafael continued.

"A Mágica?" a bewildered Pratley repeated. "Where does it come from?"

"You'll have to ask Foguinho that," smiled Rafael.

"What are you talking about?" moaned Pratley. "Can you talk English please? And who on earth is Foguinho?!"

"I am," smiled Jamie, joining the conversation.

As he looked at Colin Pratley, Jamie remembered something that Mike had told him not so long ago ... something about what you should do when you win.

"Well played, Mr Pratley," said Jamie. "You're a really good defender and it was a tough battle against you!"

Mr Pratley turned and stared at Jamie. The man looked as though he had never been given a compliment in his life.

"Yes ... well," said Mr Pratley. "Maybe there's a little bit more to your game than kick and chase."

Jamie looked at Mr Pratley. Had he just heard right? Had Pratley just said something almost nice to him? Then suddenly something else clicked in Jamie's head. When he had joined the conversation between Pratley and Rafael, he could have sworn that Rafael had been speaking without a stammer in public. Could it be?

As if to answer the question, Rafael looked at Jamie and reached out his hand.

"Here, Jamie," he said in a clear, confident voice.

Rafael was handing Jamie his notepad.

"I can look at it?" Jamie asked.

"No," said Rafael, shaking his head. "You can keep it."

"No way," said Jamie immediately. "There's no way I can keep it."

Rafael nodded. It was a firm and warm nod.

"It's yours," he said, placing the notepad into Jamie hand.

Jamie gently accepted the notepad. He knew better than anyone how much this little book meant to Rafael and how many hours he had spent pouring all of his football knowledge and ideas into it.

With hands slightly trembling, Jamie opened it.

On the first page was written:

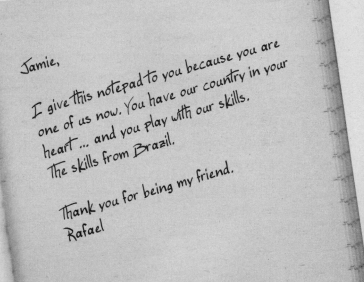

Jamie,

I give this notepad to you because you are one of us now. You have our country in your heart ... and you play with our skills. The skills from Brazil.

Thank you for being my friend.
Rafael

There were other people starting to gather around Jamie and Rafael now but it made no difference to Rafael's speech; he still carried on talking freely.

"You were right, Jamie," he said. "It still hurts, but it does get better."

Rafael and Jamie smiled at each other.

They were two football geniuses. Of a different kind.

Play On

Saturday 23 August –
five weeks later...

Bernard rested his hand lightly on Rafael's shoulder. It was very nearly time for them to go. The plane was due to take off in half an hour.

Jamie knew that he would miss Rafael so much. Everything that they had experienced over the last few months had bonded them together so closely.

After the Teachers v Pupils game and the end of term, they had spent every day of the holidays together, back in their favourite old routine: going to the park with Jack and the others until it got dark and then home to Jamie's to rule the world of football together on Soccer Manager. There wasn't a team on earth that could stop them.

Mike, who had brought Jamie to the airport to say goodbye, gave Bernard a firm handshake and Jamie saw that, once again, Bernard was smiling. Since Rafael had overcome his stutter after the match at school, Bernard looked as though the weight of a million years of worry had been lifted from his shoulders. Jamie recognized the smile too – it was just like the one in the photo in his house back in Brazil.

"Last call for Flight 2410 to Rio de Janeiro," boomed the airport announcer.

The boys knew their time was nearly up.

"Keep practising A Mágica!" said Rafael, putting his arm around Jamie after they had done a big high five. "I can't wait to tell Mestre you actually did it!"

"I will!" replied Jamie. "And if you see Arnaldo, say hi to him and tell him I'm going to be a professional one day, just like him. I believe it now … so much."

"Me too, Jamie," said Rafael. "And don't worry – I'll be following your career every step of the way."

Both Bernard and Rafael gave Jamie a final wave. Then they slowly turned to walk through the departure gate.

Jamie waved back. He body was filled with a feeling of complete warmth. He imagined Rafael going back to Brazil, speaking without a stutter and starting to build a new future with his dad. Jamie was so proud to have played his part.

But just as he considered that thought, another question jumped rapidly into Jamie's mind: in all the time that he had spent with Rafael, who, really, had been helping who?

"Rafael!" Jamie shouted, just before they disappeared.

Rafael turned around.

"*Obrigado*," said Jamie, holding up Rafael's notepad. He now carried it with him everywhere, just as Rafael had done when he'd first joined the school.

Rafael's big, warm Brazilian smile shone back at him.

"Play on, Foguinho," said Rafael. His voice rang out clear and true. "Play on…"

59

Postscript

Twenty-five years later

A press conference is being held at Hawkstone United's stadium.

A smartly dressed man walks through the door and into the room. It is full of photographers and journalists all there to hear what he has to say.

The man sits down at the table and clears his throat. He knows what he is going to say. He prepared these words all of last night. He has been preparing for this moment his entire life.

He pulls the microphone towards him and begins to speak.

"I want to say what an honour it is to be managing

in the Premier League and, in particular, here at Hawkstone United," he explains.

His voice is cool, crisp, clear and confident.

"This, for me, is a dream come true."

A sea of hands rise into the air. All the journalists want to ask him a question. The man points to a reporter in the third row.

"You've already won trophies in Brazil, Portugal and Spain, and we're delighted to have you in the Premier League now," the journalist says. "But you are the most wanted young manager in the world … you could have picked any club you liked. So why, of all the clubs in the world, have you picked Hawkstone United?"

The man smiles. A big Brazilian smile.

"Because for me, this club … this place … feels like home," says Rafael da Cruz. "In many ways, my football journey started here when I was a kid. And you are right, I did have many offers from many other clubs, but when I discussed it with my wife Rosária, and I told her how Hawkstone was the club in my heart, we decided I had to take this offer. In the end, it was the only decision we could make."

A door opens at the back of the room, and for a second, all of the photographers and cameras turn to face the phenomenal footballer who has just walked in. But Jamie Johnson is not there to steal the attention; he just wants to watch and listen like everyone else.

"And of course, there is one other very special reason that I had to take this job," Rafael da Cruz says, acknowledging the new arrival. "As a coach, you simply don't turn down the opportunity to work with a player like Jamie Johnson."

Rafael smiles and nods towards the back of the room. Jamie Johnson, captain of Hawkstone United, is smiling too. He gives his old friend and new manager a big thumbs up. Time has passed but their connection is still there. It will always be there.

"Since we were kids, I have followed Jamie's career every step of the way," says Rafael. "How he has never given up ... how he has fought back from his horrendous injuries to become the greatest player in this club's history.

"And now, together – with him as my captain – we are about to write a new chapter in Hawkstone's history ... and I hope it will be the most exciting chapter of all.

"Jamie Johnson is the man to lead and inspire my new team because he plays the game exactly how I believe it should be played: with skill, with freedom, with passion and with, if I may say, that little touch of magic..."

Top 10 Questions with Dan Freedman

1. *If I have only read* Skills From Brazil, *which Jamie Johnson books should I read next?*

Well, you've got the whole of the Jamie Johnson series to go then! Start with *The Kick Off*. But remember, it's just the beginning...

2. *Do you get much fan mail from your readers?*

Yes, what with Facebook, Twitter, my website, emails and letters, there are lots of ways for Jamie Johnson fans to get in touch with me and I always make sure I respond. Being an author, you tend to spend a fair bit of time writing on your own, so hearing from people who have read the books is always a brilliant moment. It makes all the hard work worth it!

3. *What was it like writing about Jamie before he was famous?*

It was great. At one stage, even the best footballers in the world – people like Messi and Ronaldo – were just football-mad schoolkids! So we can all empathize with Jamie's dream of making it to the top. Going back and writing a prequel was fun for me as an author too because I already know what happens to Jamie next...

4. Did you do any research about Brazil before you started writing?

I read lots of books about Brazil, its culture and its football history. It's such a fascinating country and its football history is so rich that it was a treasure trove of information and superb stories. I'm the same as Jamie: slightly obsessed with Brazilian football. It would make me really proud if some Brazilian kids read this book and liked it.

5. So is A Mágica a real skill and is it allowed in a game?

Yes and yes! I always try to include a special skill in the JJ books and I wanted this one to be particularly unique, as Jamie learns it in Brazil – the home of samba skills! So when I found this skill on the internet, I knew it was the one. It's mostly called the Seal Dribble because it involves the player balancing the ball on their head like a seal. Check it out on the internet – it's superb!

6. What's the best goal you've ever seen?

Marco van Basten bicycle kick for Ajax v Den Bosch in 1986. Check it out.

7. What's your favourite thing about writing about Jamie Johnson and who is he based on?

I get to sit and daydream about football! That's my job! I also find Jamie very intriguing as a character. I always say that, with Jamie, you're never quite sure what he's going to do. Is he going to turn around, produce a sensational bit of skill and belt one in from 35 yards? Or is he going to lose his temper, do something he regrets and get himself sent off? Characters like that keep you guessing, which is great for the readers and the author.

Jamie is partly based on me (we have a fair bit in common) and partly based on the great players I have been lucky enough to meet. People like Ronaldo, Messi, Rooney... I have taken a little bit from each of these players, added them to my own character and experiences ... and the result is Jamie Johnson. He is the kind of player I would love to see play live.

8. Which part of Skills From Brazil did you most enjoy writing?

I loved the story as a whole. The more I thought about it, the more it just seemed to sit right. I felt like my job was to tell it in the best way possible. I loved Jamie's Brazilian nickname, Foguinho – Little Fire. This was suggested to me by a Brazilian friend of mine who I worked with at the Fustal World Cup ... coming from a Brazilian football expert, I knew I had to use it! I also loved writing about the friendship between Jamie and Rafael, which grew during the story ... and how it helped give Rafael the confidence to speak freely. Even though I wrote the story and knew what was going to happen, I still felt moved at the end.

9. If you had to pick any footballer to have a kick around with, who would it be?

Good question. I've got massive respect for Steven Gerrard. He offered me his support before *The Kick Off* came out, when I was a completely unknown author, and I'll never forget that. Thierry Henry is a man full of charisma and intelligence. David Beckham and Gary Lineker are both legends as people, never mind what they have achieved in the game. Messi and Ronaldo are both taking football to a new level... But perhaps, at the moment, I would like to have a kick around with Gareth Bale. He's a left winger – like Jamie – and there are lots of similarities between their stories too, so I have a whole load of questions I need to ask him!

10. What the best game you've ever seen live?

I was lucky enough to watch the World Cup Quarter Final: Brazil v England in Japan in 2002 and then fly home on the plane to London with the England players afterwards. I'll never forget it...

Acknowledgements

Thanks to:
Mum, Ivan, Dad and Linda for all your support.

Major for your fantastic ideas.

Arnaldo Hase, Stuart Mawhinney, Chris Gerstle, Pedro Badur, Paulo Sivieri, Rowena Simmons, Ena McNamara, Hayley Katz and Martin Hitchcock for your expert advice.

Zoe King and Neil Blair for joining Jamie's team.

David Baldwin for your illustration and for teaching me how to play football! George Roberts for your tactical insights. So glad you are both part of this.

Natasha Pluckrose, Sim Parrott, Jim Dees, Jim Sells, Phillip Glyn, Jonathan Kaye, Scott Grant, Kieran Nokes, Claire Lewis, Oli Karger, Viv and Irvin for all your help.

Hazel Ruscoe – this story is inspired by ideas we had together.

Sam and Joe Talbot for making Jamie's story real.

Ms Havers – it was so much fun discussing this with you.

Lola Cashman for keeping me going all those years ago when I wanted to give up.

The brilliant Samantha Selby Smith, Jessica White, Jason Cox and the first-class team at Scholastic for everything you have done for me and Jamie Johnson.

From
Rafael's
Notepad ...

Strengths

o Quick feet
o Incredible pace
o Brave
o Great finisher
o Never gives up
o Smooth, athletic running style
o Eager to learn
o Passionate
o Superb balance
o Unique acrobatic ability
o Instinctive
o Genius left foot
o Potential to be best young player I have
  ever seen

Weaknesses

o Short temper
o Impatient
o Lack of emotional control
o Doesn't like being told what to do
o Does he know how good he is?

Mestre's A Mágica

Flick the ball up, keep eyes on the ball. Prepare to cushion the ball.

RDC

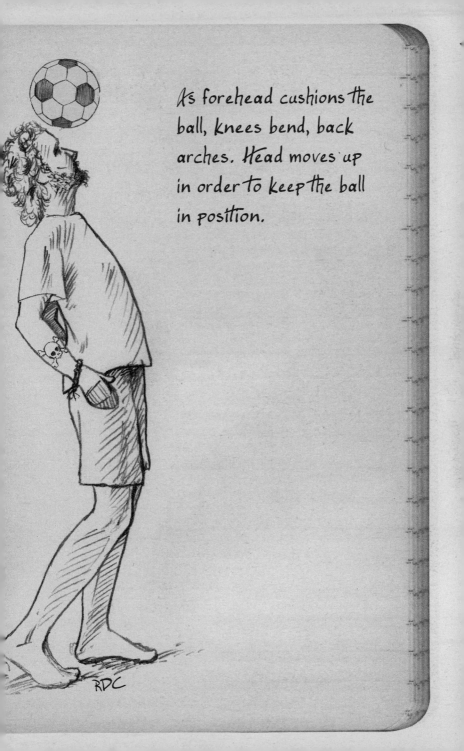

As forehead cushions the ball, knees bend, back arches. Head moves up in order to keep the ball in position.

Make sure the ball is balanced on top of the forehead. Run with the ball, tilting the head. Keep consistent speed.

Run smoothly with the ball under control. Be quick and consistent and avoid the defenders.

RDC

Speaking Football in Brazil!

English	Brazilian/Portuguese
Football	Futebol
Ball	Bola
Shot	Chute
Goal	Gol
Skill	Habilidade
Dribble	Finta
Bicycle kick	Bicicleta
Back-heel	Calcanhar
Nutmeg	Caneta
Celebration	Comemoração
Attacker	Atacante
Striker	Centro-avante
Defender	Defensor
Midfielder	Meio-Campo
Goalkeeper	Goleiro
Manager	Gerente
Team	Time
Referee	Árbitro
Free kick	Cobrança de Falta
Foul	Falta
Volley	Voleio
Header	Cabeçada
Cross	Cruzamento (noun)
	Cruzar (verb)
Offside	Impedimento
Whistle	Apito

English	Brazilian/Portuguese
Substitute	Reserva
Stadium	Estádio
Coach	Técnico
Pitch	Campo
Players	Jogadores
Penalty	Pênalti
Corner	Escanteio
Throw on	Lateral
Goal kick	Tiro de meta
Half-time	Intervalo
Full time	Final de jogo
Pass	Passe
Score a goal	Fazer o gol
Through ball	Passe em profundidade
Yellow card	Cartão amarelo
Red card	Cartão vermelho
Header	Cabeceio
Net	Rede
Trophy	Troféu
Champions	Campeões
League	Liga
World Cup	Copa do Mundo
Losers	Perdedores
Winners	Vencedores
Skills from Brazil	Habilidades do Brasil